Blind-Sided

He could see the tip of the hat brim in the doorway of the balcony across the street. Just over the top of the ridge of the mercantile store's roof, he caught a glimpse of another hat. That meant at least two men were waiting to kill him in cold blood.

Ike Murdo knows that awaiting him upon his arrival are several people who want him dead. The risks were clear when he chose to interfere with the gang's plans. He'd had no choice: when the son of the woman he loved was kidnapped, Ike followed his heart.

Now, he must pay the price and confront the gunmen.

He swallowed his fear and called out to the gunfighter. 'Cadwall! Come out and face me.'

Blind-Sided

Billy Hall

A Black Horse Western

ROBERT HALE · LONDON

© Billy Hall 2015
First published in Great Britain 2015

ISBN 978-0-7198-1628-4

Robert Hale Limited
Clerkenwell House
Clerkenwell Green
London EC1R 0HT

www.halebooks.com

The right of Billy Hall to be identified as
author of this work has been asserted by him
in accordance with the Copyright, Designs and
Patents Act 1988

Typeset by
Derek Doyle & Associates, Shaw Heath
Printed and bound in Great Britain by
CPI Antony Rowe, Chippenham and Eastbourne

CHAPTER 1

He knew the boots would draw comments. No matter. They were far more comfortable for walking than his riding boots.

That's why he always carried both with him. Cowboy boots were torture if a man was going to be on his feet for any length of time. On the other hand, he well knew that in cow country, anyone not wearing riding boots was 'a town guy,' a 'green horn,' or 'some dirt farmer'.

Town guys were accepted. After all, nobody expected the bartender, or the clerk at the mercantile store, to be wearing riding boots. Green horns were . . . well . . . they were just green horns. Anyone else riding into town with different footwear was regarded with suspicion.

Ike Murdo bellied up to the bar at Kelsey's Saloon. There were, surprisingly, three to choose from on the main street of Chickasaw.

The Pleasure Palace appeared to him to be more dominantly a whore house than a saloon, not to mention pretty swank for a cow town. That meant the drinks would be twice the price of the other places, and about half water.

Hank's Saloon looked to be shabby and poorly maintained, so he guessed it would be the hangout of the rough crowd. He chose Kelsey's as the best gamble.

By the time he had walked from the door to the bar, he knew his footwear had already been well assessed. 'What'll you have?' the broad-faced bartender greeted.

'Whiskey, if you've got some good stuff.'

'How good you want?'

'Not the stuff the mayor drinks. I'm a workin' man.'

The bartender grinned. 'The mayor ain't likely to drink here. He sorta favors the Pleasure Palace.'

'Likes the good stuff, well watered down, huh?'

The bartender's grin broadened. 'You know him, do you?'

'Nope. Just guessin'.'

'Not bad for a guess,' the bartender said as he filled the shot glass. 'Want me to leave the bottle?'

'No, one'll most likely be plenty.'

'Gimme a yell if you want a refill.'

'Will do. Anyone hirin' around?'

The bartender's face clouded. 'Not many. Been awful dry the last couple years. This year especially. Most places have cut down their herds.'

'It does look awful dry, all right.'

'It's purty bad. Oh, we get a shower now and again, but we're in bad need of a few good frog-drowners. The churches in town are even startin' to have prayer meetin's to pray for rain.'

'Better be careful what they pray for. Someone just might be a-listenin'.'

The barkeep chuckled. 'I went to one the other night.

6

Even Old Ned Haskins was there. First time anyone ever remembered him even bein' in a church. Ned, he's plumb hard hearin'. I guess he figgers everyone else is too. When he talks you can hear 'im three miles upwind on a breezy day. The preacher opened it up for anyone to pray what wanted to. Old Ned, by gum, stood right up an' prayed. Right out loud. And I do mean loud. Don't guess the Lord had any trouble hearin' him. And he says, "Lord, send us some rain. Now don't go givin' us one them gol-danged rip-roarin' rains that washes out more stuff than it waters. Give us one o' them long, slow, drizzle-drazzles that lasts a couple or three weeks".'

Ike chuckled his appreciation of the word picture the bartender painted. He had no idea whether it had any basis in fact, or whether the bartender actually went to a prayer meeting, but he had to admit it made a good story.

As the bartender moved off in response to someone's signal for more drinks, Ike moved to a table against the rear wall. He leaned back in his chair and surveyed the patrons of the saloon.

It did not escape his attention that three men at one table had taken special notice of him. Their conversation obviously centered on him. He ignored them.

The largest of the three finally caught his eye and motioned him over. Not sure whether he was about to be the recipient of a friendly gesture or the object of something less agreeable, he rose and walked over to the table.

'Evenin', boys,' he greeted.

'Where you from?' one of the cowboys inquired. 'Ain't seen you around here before.'

'Just rode in today. Lookin' for work. You boys know

7

anyone that's hirin'?'

'You ain't ax'ly gonna try to hire out as a cowhand wearin' dirt farmer boots, are you?'

Ike looked down at his shoes. 'Well, that depends, I guess.'

'On what?'

'On whether I ride out there or walk. If I'm gonna walk, these boots are a whole lot easier on the feet.'

All three men snorted as if they'd just heard something vulgar. 'Where you gonna go on foot, lookin' for a ranch job?'

Ike shrugged. 'All depends. I do like to walk. If a place ain't more'n five or six miles, I just might walk an' let my horse rest.'

The three looked at each other as if they'd just heard the most absurd bit of nonsense since *Goldilocks and The Three Bears*. The first one that had spoken said, 'Anybody that'd walk instead o' ride when he's got a choice, sure ain't no cowpoke. Ain't much of a man either, if you ask me.'

Ike smiled. 'Well, I didn't ask you, but since you offered me the benefit of your ignorance anyway, I'd have to say that anyone that judges another man by the cut of his boots ain't too sure of his own manhood.'

The cowboy reddened instantly. 'You sayin' I ain't sure if I'm a man?'

Ike's smile widened. 'If you were, you wouldn'ta stayed sittin' over here all protected by your friends when you challenged me.'

The cowboy's response was instantaneous. He swiftly swung a massive fist in an attempt to connect with Ike's groin before he expected it.

Ike was more than ready for the sucker punch. He turned sideways, letting the other man's fist plunge through empty air. At the same time he grabbed the man by the shirt and jerked. The momentum of his swing coupled with Ike's surprising strength propelled him out of the chair, sprawling him headlong into the sawdust that covered the floor.

He whirled over and lunged to standing. Just as he gained his feet, Ike sent a hard right that landed on the point of his chin. He sprawled in the sawdust again, this time on his back.

He was both tough and quick. He rolled away and came to his feet again, shaking his head to clear it. Before he had time to get set or aim a punch, however, another rock hard fist flattened his nose and sent him back to the sawdust.

He came to his feet instantly again, lunging toward his adversary as he did so. Once again Ike seemed to intuit the move before it began. He sidestepped and landed a smashing right to the man's ear as he tried in vain to keep his balance. He plowed face first into the sawdust once again.

He came up more slowly the next time, giving Ike time to plant a solid left to his cheekbone. Part of his fist caught the heavy brow of his right eye, ripping open a long gash.

As he struggled to his feet, blood flowed into and over his right eye. Deliberately staying to that side of him, where his vision was hampered, Ike sent three short chopping blows into his face. Then he once again sent an overhand right to the point of his chin. When he hit the sawdust for the fifth time, he stayed where he fell.

Ike turned to the man's companions, sitting with mouths agape. He smiled at them, as if they were having a casual conversation. 'Do either one of you fellas want to try your hand at an old farm boy?'

He was still breathing easily. The only mark on him was the blood on his knuckles. None of it was his. Both men declined the offer. 'You made your point,' one of them said. 'Too bad you ain't wearin' a gun. I'd see if you're as good with it as you are with your fists.'

'Now why would you wanta do that?' Ike asked, as if it were a new and strange idea.

The man he had beaten was struggling to his feet. Without saying anything more, the pair at the table moved to help him up. They supported him between them and made their way out the door.

As Ike sat back down at his table, the bartender appeared with the bottle of whiskey. 'Refill's on the house,' he offered. 'Ain't often anyone manages to stand up to Kruger's boys.'

Ike held up his hand. 'Thanks, but one's enough.'

'You said somethin' about bein' a farm boy,' the barkeep said. 'Do you mind doin' some farmin' along with cowpunchin'?'

Ike shook his head. 'Not a bit. I cut my eye teeth walkin' behind a plow. Are there actually folks around here that do some farmin'?'

The barman nodded. 'Actually, Kruger does, but he doesn't do all that good a job of it. The place on down the crick from him – the U-V-Cross ranch – does more. Place is run by the widow Vogel. She expects her hands to be good cowhands. She runs six or seven hundred head. But she expects 'em to fix fences around the corn field too, and farm it, and put up hay. She won't hire anyone that thinks he can do all his work from the saddle.'

'Makes sense,' Ike opined. 'Seems like awful dry country to farm, though.'

'She irrigates from the crick, same as Kruger does. Anyhow, you might see if she's hirin'. She has a harder time gettin' good hands, 'cause she figgers they all oughta like farmin' an' fencin' just as much as they do punchin' cows.'

'I'll give it a shot,' Ike promised. Then he grinned. 'It just might keep a man from gettin' bored with doin' the same thing all the time.'

CHAPTER 2

'Hi, mister. Are you lookin' for a job?'

Laugh lines crinkled at the corners of Ike Murdo's eyes, but his face betrayed no expression. 'Well, as a matter of fact, I am. Are you hirin'?'

Seven-year-old Billy Vogel looked him up and down as if appraising a horse. 'Well, maybe. If you don't mind farmin' some. We don't hire nobody what won't do fencin' an' plowin'.'

'Is that a fact? That's a little unusual in cow country, ain't it?'

'Yup. That's why we don't just hire any ol' drifter that comes ridin' in.'

'Well, that's good. I don't guess I'd wanta work for a place that did.'

'You ain't runnin' from the law or nothin', are you?'

'Billy!' an imperious voice from the porch of the house called. 'Will you get in here? Right now!'

'Aw, Ma, I was just checkin' out this guy what's lookin' for work.'

Ike tagged along behind the boy as he reluctantly

responded to his mother's command. She looked at him apologetically. 'I'm sorry. Billy gets a little big for his britches sometimes.'

Ike grinned. 'Oh, I don't know. He was doin' a pretty good job of asking me all the right questions.'

Billy shot him a grateful look before he slow-poked his way through the door. His mother offered only a rueful smile. 'I don't know if they were the right questions, but I'm sure he asked you a lot of them.'

'He seems like a mighty bright boy.'

'He's a handful,' Minerva Vogel acknowledged. 'If you are looking for work, you'll need to talk to my foreman, Ross. He's on his way across the yard now.'

Ike tipped his hat to the lady. 'I'm much obliged, ma'am. By the way, my name's Ike Murdo.'

'Short for Isaiah?'

'Yes ma'am. That's actually my middle name, though. I don't often admit to my first name.'

'It couldn't be worse than Minerva,' she grinned.

'Well, it ain't as bad as if I was named Minerva,' he quipped, 'but for a fine homely woman, I'd call that a right nice name.'

'Homely?' she shot back, eyebrows arched. Her tone left no question whether the term irritated her.

He sobered, confusion etched on his face. 'Ain't that a good word? To call a lady, I mean?'

'Not usually, if you really want to know.'

'Well, I'm sure beggin' your pardon then. I sure didn't mean to offend. My folks, they used that word a lot, describin' women-folk that was good at makin' a home for their family. They always meant it kindly.'

13

'Really? I guess I hadn't heard it used that way. When I've heard it used, it means someone that isn't very good looking. One step above ugly, even.'

'Really?' It was his turn to marvel. 'Boy, I sure never heard it used like that. If I had, I absolutely would not have even thought of it describing you. You very definitely wouldn't fit that meaning of the word. You're downright beautiful, in fact. Beggin' your pardon, ma'am. I . . . I didn't mean to sound forward.'

Her eyes twinkled and danced at his sudden discomfiture. 'You look more like you're embarrassed than forward. But thank you for the compliment.'

She motioned toward the man who had walked up beside Ike. 'Mr Murdo, this is Ross Endicott. He's my foreman. Ross, I believe this blushing gentleman is looking for work.'

Making a valiant attempt to avoid looking as foolish as he felt, Ike thrust a hand out to the foreman. 'Glad to meet you,' he said. 'I am lookin' for a job.'

'I think Billy interrogated him pretty well already,' Minerva grinned, 'so I'll go back in the house and let you start all over.'

Ross nodded. Ike tipped his hat to her again. When the door closed behind her, he turned to the foreman. With a grin he said, 'Billy tells me you don't hire anyone that ain't willin' to farm an' fence.'

Ross watched him closely as he responded. 'That boy doesn't miss much. I 'spect he either got that from his ma or from me. Coulda been either one, I guess.'

Ike glanced back in the direction from which he had come. 'Ridin' in I did notice some ground that sure

14

oughta be gettin' plowed by now.'

'Where you from?'

'Ohio.'

'Was you in the war?'

Ike nodded. 'Forty-second Ohio Infantry, under Garfield's command.'

'You made it through in one piece, I see.'

'Yeah. We didn't lose as many men as a lot o' units did. Lost our share, though.'

'Why'd you come West?'

Ike shrugged. 'Farther away from the war. Better chances to get ahead out here. Wyoming's still pretty new country. I was surprised to see land bein' farmed here, though. Pretty short growin' season, ain't it?'

'Not as bad as you'd s'pose, most o' the time. Here in the valley, anyway. Up higher it would be. We don't usually have any trouble gettin' a corn crop. Water's the only problem.'

'I seen a lot o' windmills.'

Ross nodded. 'Yup. Finest invention there ever was for cow-calf operations. We still got a couple Halladays. Got a couple Wheeler solid wheel ones. Mostly, now, we're goin' to them new Aermotors. They'll pull water up from a couple hundred feet, if you gotta go that deep to hit water. Gotta have 'em for the cattle. The crick ain't enough to water as many cattle as we got. It ain't all that dependable, after we get done usin' it for irrigation, anyway.'

'Ah! You use it to irrigate the corn.'

'Yup. Then what's left over we use on the hay meadows. It takes a heap o' hay in the winter for as many cows as we run.'

Ike frowned. 'If you use up all the water for the corn and hay, what do the folks downstream from you do for water?'

Ross grinned. 'There ain't no downstream on Hatfield Crick.'

Ike frowned in total confusion. 'What do you mean?'

'Just one o' them freaks o' nature, I guess. She's a mighty fine crick afore it gets to Kruger's place. He gets to use half the water. Then it runs through U-V-Cross, but afore it gets to the other end o' the place, it hits the sand flats. It just sorta spreads out there an' disappears.'

'Disappears?'

'Just plumb disappears. Drains right into the ground. There ain't even no crick-bed on past the sand flats, so I don't guess it ever did run no farther.'

'You don't say! I never heard o' such a thing. How big are the sand flats?'

'Oh, they ain't all that big. Maybe a mile long, half that wide. Fine sand as deep as you wanta dig. It looks like it mighta been some sort o' lake bed, once upon a time. That'd be a long time afore there was any two-legged critters around to look at it, though.'

'Well what d'ya know,' Ike mused.

'Well, I know we ain't gettin' to the subject at hand none too quick. We do need another hand or two. But like little Billy told ya, workin' this spread means ya gotta be a full-blown cow poke one day an' fix fence or work the farm ground the next.'

Ike smiled. 'I heard that in town, before I rode out here. To tell the truth, I kinda like the sound o' that. I grew up walkin' behind a plow. Lot different soil than

16

here, but I'm guessin' it don't slide through the ground any easier here.'

Ross bobbed his head. 'You'll hit a rock or two once in a while. Well, the fact is, you'll hit a rock o' some sort about every five or six feet. But it grows almost as good o' corn as it does rocks.'

'You fence the corn off from the cows, I noticed.'

'Yup.'

'Barbed wire.' It sounded like something between a statement and an accusation.

'Yup. We don't use the vicious barbs, though. We used to, 'cause that was about all there was to be had. There ain't hardly any o' that left now. We use the two-point Glidden wire now. It's still got barbs enough to keep the stock out've the corn, but the barbs ain't sharp-pointed like the vicious wire. A man can handle it without gettin' all cut to pieces.'

'If there's that many rocks in the ground, diggin' post holes has gotta be a chore.'

There wasn't really any humor in Ross's smile. 'Oh, I 'spect you might say that. Most post holes end up bein' about the size of a wash tub by the time you move enough rocks to get 'em deep enough. Most o' the boys try to do most anything there is, short o' breakin' a leg, to get outa fencin'.'

'Well, I wouldn't wanta make a livin' doin' it, but I sure don't mind takin' my turn an' doin' my share.'

Ross nodded, obviously already having made up his mind. 'The pay's thirty a month an' found. We buy ammunition for your guns an' incidentals you gotta have. You got any footwear other than them ridin' boots?'

Ike grinned. 'Yeah, I got reg'lar workin' boots that I wear when I ain't ridin'.'

'Why'd that strike you funny?'

'Oh, there was a fella in town that sorta thought they was somethin' he oughta take exception to. We kinda had a little discussion about that.'

'That so? Didn't happen to get the fella's name, by chance?'

'Devlin, I think.'

Ross's eyebrows rose considerably. 'You had a set-to with Big Dan Devlin? I don't see no marks on ya.'

Ike shrugged his huge shoulders. 'I didn't see any reason to let him mark me up.'

'I'm hopin' he don't look so good today.'

Ike shrugged again. 'Likely not. His friends pretty much carried him out.'

'Well, we'll see if you can do that good a job with a plow, about tomorrow. Put your horse up and haul your stuff over to the bunkhouse. Cook shack's hooked on to the end of it. Ling'll be clangin' that dinner bell afore long. I'll introduce you to the rest o' the crew at supper.'

Well, I got a job before I came close to runnin' outa money. Sure a lot different from what I expected, though. Might be sorta nice to do different stuff. Even if cowboys ain't supposed to like dirt farmin', Ike mused as he led his horse to the barn. *Besides, Minerva sure is one nice lookin' lady. Mighty nice, in fact.*

CHAPTER 3

Ross introduced Ike to the rest of the single men of the crew when they were all seated around the long table in the chow hall. Each of the hands offered a short word of greeting in response as Ross introduced them. The only one who didn't say anything was the one Ross introduced as 'Stutterin' Leroy'. He just lifted a hand in acknowledgment of the introduction and went on eating.

The term made Ike vaguely uncomfortable, but he didn't see any indication of discomfort in either him or any of the other hands.

There wasn't much conversation until the meal was about over. Then it mostly centered on what each of the hands was assigned to start out the next morning's work doing, who got bucked off his horse unexpectedly, whose horse had come up lame that day, and the inevitable discussion of the weather, especially the length and severity of the drought.

Ike's discomfort over Ross's introduction of 'Stutterin' Leroy' resurfaced later when the crew had all retired to the bunkhouse.

Someone had overheard the fact that Ike had whipped Big Dan Devlin in town. That led into several of the hands' descriptions of surprising outcomes to fights they had witnessed.

When that subject was well covered and conversation lagged, Slim Wilkins said, 'Hey, Leroy. Did you ever try talkin' to someone else that stuttered like you do?'

Stuttering Leroy looked up from the hackamore he was braiding. Instead of trying to answer, he just bobbed his head.

'How'd that go?' someone else asked, grinning in expectation.

Leroy looked around the bunkhouse. Every hand had stopped what they were doing, looked at him just as expectantly. He laid the half-finished hackamore aside. He clearly knew this was going to take a while. It was just as obvious there was no apprehension on his part.

He knew every hand there except Ike. He knew they were his friends, so the request wasn't an attempt to belittle him or mock him. He also knew every bunkhouse pulses with the life of the stories the cowhands shared.

'W-w . . . Once I did,' he said. 'B-b-blacksmith at D-D-Dubois.'

'The blacksmith at Dubois stuttered like you?' Tubby queried, unfolding his lank frame and leaning forward from the edge of his bunk.

'Y-Yup. W-w-worse.'

'Are you tellin' us he stuttered worse'n you do?'

'Y-Yup.'

'So what happened?'

'W-W-Well, m-m-my horse b-b-busted a shoe. S-so I went

to ha-ha-have him shod.'

'Makes sense.'

'I g-g-got off my h-h-horse. H-H-He threw down a h-h-horseshoe on the ground and w-w-walked o-o-over to me. And he says, 'C-C-Can I he-he-help y-y-you?''

Every hand in the bunkhouse watched Leroy expectantly, not sure what to ask or how to respond. After a long silence, Leroy said, 'S-S-So I just g-g-got back on my h-h-horse and r-r-rode away.'

Another profound silence held the room for a long moment as each man digested the implications of Leroy's story. Then scattered laughter and a flurry of explanations erupted.

'Well, what else could you do?'

'If you'd tried to answer 'im, he'da thought you was makin' fun of 'im, sure's sin!'

'If you'da tried to answer 'im, he'da busted your head afore you could get a whole word spit out.'

'If you're gonna have someone think you're makin' fun of 'im, it sure better not be a blacksmith. Them guys is stouter'n a bull!'

'Some of 'em have a temper just as bad, too,' one cowboy offered. 'The smithy where I grew up had the worst temper I ever seen. If somethin' went wrong he'd start cussin' a blue streak an' throwin' stuff around. By the time he cooled off, his hammers an' half his tools would be layin' out in the street in front of his blacksmith shop.'

'That'd be a hard guy to do business with.'

'Harder yet to work for.'

'You worked for him?'

'No, but a friend o' mine did.'

'For how long?'

'Oh, quite a while.'

'How'd he manage to keep the guy from gettin' mad at him?'

'Well, when he hired out, the smith kept tellin' 'im over an' over that he didn't wanta have to tell 'im every little thing to do. He needed to see what he was workin' on, figure out what he needed, and just jump in an' help with whatever it was he was doin'.'

'Makes sense.'

'Yup. It was about the second or third day on the job; the smith went an' blew his stack over somethin'. He started cussin' a blue streak like usual, an' throwin' his stuff out the door. Glen – that's my friend's name – he started cussin' a blue streak too, an' throwin' stuff out the door just like the blacksmith was. It just took a minute for the blacksmith to stop an' stare at 'im. Then he yelled, 'What in the Sam Hill do you think you're doin'?' Glen he says, "I'm helpin' ya with what you're doin', just like you said." '

About half the hands erupted with laughter. The others stared at the storyteller, to find out whether it cooled the blacksmith off or got Glen beaten. Before it could be explained, a steady string of blacksmith stories vied with each other for the funniest or the oddest or the most amazing.

Ike lay back on his bunk, enjoying the repartee and easy camaraderie of the crew. *I think I lucked out an' hired on to a good outfit*, he told himself as he drifted off to sleep.

CHAPTER 4

The darker of the two horses was named Duke. It only stood to reason that the mare would be called Duchess. She was almost a hand shorter than Duke.

Ike was in love with the matched Percherons before he even got the harnesses buckled on. They both snuffled him curiously, and evidently decided he was acceptable. The larger of the two even turned his head around and nuzzled him in the ribs when he was brushing him down. As he moved around them, each of them moved away from the edge of the stall to allow him room. 'Somebody's sure done a good job with teachin' this team,' he muttered.

When they were curried, grained, and harnessed, he led them to where the plow sat waiting for its first work of the season. The team walked past it, then backed up to it as if they had done so a hundred times before. He hitched them to it, pondering the plow quizzically.

Only now did the comments of Al Reynolds, the ranch's blacksmith and handyman, make sense. 'I got 'er all greased up an' ready to go for ya,' he had said.

At the time his remark didn't make sense. There was nothing except the lathe to grease on any plow he had ever used. A plow's solid framework was immovably connected to the moldboard. The depth to which a field was plowed was regulated by how high or low he held the handles while the horse pulled it.

Now he stood before the plow he was supposed to know how to operate. It bore little resemblance to any he had ever used.

He did notice with approval the heavy coating of grease that covered the plow's lathes. *That's old grease,* he observed. *It was put on there when they were done with it last year. I ain't even gonna have to fight rust to get it to start scourin'.*

He scratched the back of his neck as he looked over the plow. 'Now why don't you two nags tell me how to use this thing?' he commented to the equine pair. 'I gotta figure out how to use the danged thing without lookin' like a green horn idiot.'

The plow was two-bottomed, something that was totally new to him. 'Imagine, plowin' two furrows at the same time!' he muttered. Duchess ignored the comment. Duke at least turned his head and looked at him. He blew softly. It sure sounded like he was mocking this new hand.

Well, it was obvious where he was supposed to sit. That in itself was new and different. Every mile of field he had plowed – and there were a good many – he had plowed walking behind the plow, gripping the twin handles until his arms and shoulders ached beyond endurance.

He climbed on to the seat and toyed with the tall levers. It was relatively obvious how to raise and lower the moldboards, and how to lock the levers into position to maintain the depth at which he needed to plow.

Ross's comment when he had assigned him plowing duty that day finally made sense. He had said, 'You'll likely wanta plow at about four notches. Over in the swale the ground's heavier, so you'll likely need to raise it a notch there.'

'Hyup,' he told the team, picking up the reins.

Once again, as if knowing far better than he where they were going, they headed in the direction where he had noted the barbed wire fence upon his arrival. He hadn't noticed the location of the gate that allowed entry. He assumed the team knew where it was. Sure enough, they walked directly to it.

He opened the gate, pulling it clear around against the fence. He left it there where there was no danger of a horse tangling in the wire. The team didn't bother to wait for him. They pulled the plow forward without any command from him. As soon as the plow was clear of the gate they stopped and waited. He climbed back up on to the seat. There would be no need to close it until the plowing and planting of the corn was done.

He maneuvered the team to a corner of the field. It would be more accurate to say the team maneuvered him to direct them to where he was supposed to begin. 'Looks like you two know more about what we're doin' than I do,' he admitted.

He sat there feeling like a green tinhorn for several heartbeats. There were two levers, one to lower each of the moldboards. He had two hands. That was an appropriate match. 'I got that much figured out right outa the gate,' he complimented himself sarcastically.

But there were also the reins. How was he supposed to hold the reins and operate both levers at the same time? Should he lower the moldboards before the team started, or as they started? Should he drop them clear to the fourth notch, as Ross had suggested, right away, or slowly?

Duke and Duchess grew tired of the delay. They started moving along the edge of the field. Not knowing what else to do, Ike stuck the reins in his mouth, gripping them with his teeth. He squeezed the release handles on the levers and pushed, lowering them. As they reached the fourth notch, he released the grips, letting the flat piece of iron on each one drop into its proper notch.

He looked back over his shoulder. The reddish-brown soil was already rolling off the moldboards as if they had been polished by half a mile of furrow.

The team leaned into the harness and moved confidently forward. One of the plow lathes struck a big rock buried deep beneath the ground. That moldboard lifted up and over it, lifting the right wheel of the plow off the ground. It came back to earth with a jerk that nearly bounced Ike off the seat. The team didn't break stride, acting as if that were perfectly normal.

He soon found that it was. Rocks were regularly rolled up by the plow, or held their ground and bounced the plow up and over. 'I bet Dane's kept busy fixin' plow lathes,' he grumbled.

At the end of the field he pulled the levers back, lifting the plow lathes out of the ground. As if it were their signal, the team walked a wide circle and moved back on to the field at its very edge. Ike was able to lower the lathes again almost quickly enough to avoid a piece of unplowed ground at the corner. The team continued their pace, pulling the plow along the edge of the field at right angles to the twin furrows already plowed.

At each corner they repeated the drill. By the time they had finished the first round Ike was almost getting comfortable with the routine.

He plowed for nearly three hours. 'You two oughta be needin' a drink,' he decided.

As they drew even with the gate he raised the plow lathes out of the ground and tugged on the reins, pulling to one side. Once again the team understood what was expected. They headed for the yard and stopped in front of the water trough.

Ike climbed down and began pumping the handle. After three or four pumps, water began to gush from the spout. For a while the horses drank as fast as he could pump.

When they slowed down enough that the trough was full, he walked to the barn. He returned with two feed bags filled with oats. He buckled one on the head of each animal. They eagerly scarfed down the treat, then looked at him expectantly. Following their 'orders,' he removed the feedbags. They drank deeply again, nearly emptying the trough.

They returned to the field and turned over the rocky soil until Ling Lee clanged the iron triangle, calling the crew to dinner.

Before he went in to eat, Ike watered the team again, then turned them into the corral. He forked them a generous feed of hay, confident that they had done all the

27

day's work that would be asked of them.

He was right. But he wasn't quite ready for what came next. From across the table, Ross said, 'Tubby, you can hitch up the Belgians an' take over the plowin' for the rest o' the day. We don't want this new guy to think he's gonna get paid to sit on his duff on that plow all the time. Slim, you an' Ike can hitch Liz an' Jezebel to the stone sled an' start workin' on the rocks.'

Liz and Jezebel, Ike soon learned, were as big a team of mules as he had seen. They stood nearly sixteen hands. 'Watch Jezebel,' Slim warned as they began to harness the pair. 'She ain't got that name for nothin'. She'll be docile till you get careless. Then she'll kick ya inta the middle o' next week, just plumb outa the blue.'

The stone sled – they called it a sledge in Ohio – was something he was all too familiar with. It was nothing more than a flat platform of planks mounted on a pair of broad runners, with a double-tree to which a team could be hitched. The mules pulled it along as the men picked up the rocks the plow had turned up and loaded them on to it. In Ohio it had taken most of a field to supply enough rocks to be worth hauling out. Here it took one trip across the field.

Slim and Tubby were the constant example of cowboys' dry wit. They were almost inseparable, usually working together on the place. Tubby was nearly six feet tall and thin as a rail. Slim would've had to stand on tiptoe to make five-foot-six, but he was built like a brick. The crew joked that it was easier to jump over him than to walk around. The afternoon turned into an unspoken contest between him and Ike to see which man could lift the largest rock and load it on to the sledge without help. It was an even match.

When Slim picked up the reins and guided the mules out through the gate, Ike finally asked the question that had been rattling around in his mind. 'How come you put the rocks all along the outside o' the fence thataway?' He indicated the row of rocks, almost amounting to a rock wall in places, around the outside of the field.

'Keep the cattle away,' Slim explained. 'They like to use the posts to rub on. Especially the bulls. They think they're just put there for them to scratch with. They put so much weight agin' 'em we spend all our time replacin' posts. We're usin' the rocks to sorta make a wall that'll keep 'em away from the fence.'

They added considerably to that rock barrier before the sun got low enough to call it a day. Ike wasn't sure he'd be able to get out of bed, come morning. He did manage to overhear Slim tell the foreman, 'I don't know if he's any kind o' cowhand, but that new guy's a sure-'nough worker. He dang near worked me inta the ground tryin' to keep up with 'im.'

CHAPTER 5

'Hey, Farm Boy, we got a half-dozen horses cut outa the remuda for your string. Today'd be a good day to check 'em out. See if they suit ya.'

Ike managed to keep from smiling. With the most innocent look he could manage, he asked, 'Did you pick some nice gentle ones that are well broke?'

One of the hands looked at his feet quickly. Two others turned away, suddenly needing to check on something in the distance. The other four watched him with faces that would have done justice to any poker table. 'Oh, I don't think you'll have a problem with any of 'em,' Tubby White said in his quiet southern drawl. His stick-thin figure leaned against the wall in a valiant effort at looking casual. 'You might wanta wear your ridin' boots today, though, 'stead o' them farmin' ones you been a-wearin'.'

Ike nodded. 'That'll be a good change,' he said. 'I ain't done much but plow an' plant corn since I got here. That an' pick rocks. I ain't never seen that many rocks in one field in my life.'

'That's the best crop we grow every year, all right. If we

find a market for rocks, we'll all be rich.'

Everybody around the table seemed more than usually interested in Ike at breakfast. He pretended not to notice. He deliberately dawdled over his food, watching with increasing enjoyment the impatience of the crew.

Finally Slim Wilkins could stand it no longer. 'You sure are takin' a long time stowin' away that breakfast! Would you get a move on?'

Ike smiled. Continuing his wide-eyed innocent mien, he said, 'Oh. Sure. I'm done eatin' anyway, I guess. I didn't realize you was waitin' for me.'

'Well I think Ross had Stutterin' Leroy put your rig on one o' the horses. We just need to get goin' so we can start workin' stock in for spring roundup. Sorta holdin' up the whole crew, you know, till you're fixed up with a string o' horses an' ready to ride.'

With Slim in the lead, Ike walked about half his normal pace. From the corner of his eye he spotted the rest of the crew, all intent on some imponderable task that seemed to demand their single-minded concentration.

Tethered close to the snubbing post in the round corral, a big Appaloosa gelding stood with Ike's saddle and bridle already in place. He looked over the animal with approval. At over fourteen hands, he was a magnificent animal. A broad chest and thick neck bespoke strength and stamina. His legs were heavier than most, giving him an almost stolid appearance.

Though snubbed up uncomfortably close, he didn't fight against the restraints. Instead he watched every movement around him with quick eyes. His ears were forward and alert, without fear.

'That is one fine lookin' horse,' Ike said with approval as he stepped into the corral, closing the gate behind him. 'What is he, about a three-year-old?'

Ross nodded. 'Strong three.'

'I wonder why nobody's cabbaged on to him already,' Ike pondered.

Ross coughed as if something suddenly caught in his throat. 'Aw, I 'spect 'cause he's kinda heavy in the legs, maybe. Not likely to be as fast as most o' the boys like. Step up on 'im, an' see how he responds to ya.'

A child just starting his third reader couldn't have missed the excitement in the air. All the hands who had been so busily engrossed in something or other were now climbing on to the top rail of the corral. Unnatural silence gripped the crew. Ross watched with intense interest. In spite of it all, Ike seemed blissfully unaware of anything out of the ordinary.

As he approached the horse he asked, 'What's his name, Ross?'

Another fit of coughing prevented Ross's immediate answer. As soon as he had it under control he said, 'Oh, I don't guess he's got one, yet,' he explained. 'Not official, anyway. Most fellas like to name the horses in their string themselves.'

Well, that probably means his name's Dynamite, or Widow-Maker, or Sky-Buster, Ike told himself silently.

As he reached for the tightly secured reins, the horse's ears flattened back against his head. His eyes followed every motion Ike made, but he made no move. As Ike rubbed a hand along his neck and scratched his ear, he appeared not to notice. The hide didn't twitch. He

32

showed no fear of this stranger whatever. That in itself rang warning bells in Ike's mind.

There ain't a doubt in his mind that he's gonna take care o' me in a heartbeat, then he can go on about his business, he thought.

He checked the cinch to be sure Ross had it good and tight. Ross gripped the bridle just above the bit, holding the big animal's head firmly against the snubbing post, while trying hard to make it appear casual. As Ike stepped toward the saddle, the horse's left hind leg shot out and back in a vicious kick that would probably have broken Ike's leg if he hadn't been expecting it. He gripped the stirrup and turned it around so he could put his foot in it while staying out of reach of that eager hind hoof. He swung into the saddle, thrust his foot in the off stirrup, twisted his toes outward and hooked his spurs in the cinch.

Gripping the reins tightly he nodded to Ross. Ross released the gelding and stepped back.

Dynamite would have been an apt name.

Sky-Buster would be equally appropriate.

A long string of more colorful names had surely been attached to him.

The horse leaped straight into the air, humped his back, twisted a half turn, and hit the ground with a bone-jarring jolt. As he left the ground again he twisted in the opposite direction, then reversed it in mid-jump. His front feet hit the ground first as he kicked toward one side with both hind feet. As his hind feet connected with the ground he spun a full circle, then leaped back into the air as he once again reversed directions.

When Ike stayed with him the first couple jumps, the

crew, now perched on the top rail of the corral, whooped. With every jump of the fiercely bucking animal the tone of their yells and comments took on a more and more approving, then admiring tone.

Ike couldn't remember riding a harder bronc. He was incredibly strong and more agile than any horse looking that stocky should have possibly been. He was also extremely smart. When he had exhausted his considerable repertoire of moves, tricks and power-plays, he recognized his rider was more than a match for him. He stopped bucking in half the time Ike expected, but was not in the least winded.

Ike touched him with the spurs. He shot across the corral as if flung from a catapult. At the last instant Ike pulled his head to one side to force him to turn the way he wanted. He did. He spun on a dime and offered Ike nine cents in change. In one jump he was back at full speed, heading for the other side of the corral.

They repeated the action three more times, then Ike abruptly pulled his head to the side halfway across the corral. It confused the horse momentarily. He made three stiff-legged jumps the way he had been moving, with his head pulled to the side. Then he relented to the reins' insistence and turned the way he was being hauled.

To Ike's surprise he did not start bucking again in frustration. But he did run! That horse was quicker and faster than any horse Ike could remember riding. After four times pulling him to one side with the reins, the horse caught on, and began responding as soon as the reins were moved.

Ike kept the reins to the side, and the horse stayed in

the center of the corral, spinning around three complete turns before Ike straightened him out again.

The loudest cheer yet emanated from the assembled crew. No man among them would expect that kind of response from a bronc being ridden for the first time.

When Ike pulled back on the reins the gelding fought against them briefly, then squatted his hind legs and stopped in his tracks, without the bone-jarring jolts delivered by horses that used their front legs to stop. Ike leaped from the saddle, ready for the animal to kick at him, attempt to bite him, or otherwise vent his animosity. He did none of the expected. Instead he turned to face Ike and stood there eyeing him, with his ears forward and his head low. He tossed his head once, then began a chewing motion with his jaw.

'Well, would you lookit that!' somebody's voice on the fence echoed his own thoughts. 'He already decided to let him be the boss.'

'You are some kinda horse, fella,' Ike said in a soothing voice. 'I ain't never heard of a horse catchin' on to stuff that fast.'

As Ross walked across the corral, Ike demanded, 'Did he used to belong to someone?'

'Nope.'

'It sure ain't the first time anyone forked 'im!'

'It ain't the first time anyone tried,' Ross admitted. 'Every hand in the place has tried a time or two. Ain't nobody stayed with him more'n two or three jumps, though. I ain't never seen any horse anywhere take to neck-reinin' thataway.'

'Me neither,' Ike agreed. 'An' he ain't even breathin'

35

hard! I'm breathin' a lot harder'n he is.'

'Dangdest thing I ever saw,' Ross marveled. 'So what're ya gonna call 'im?'

'Mine!' Ike said without thinking.

Ross chuckled. 'Yeah, he's sure enough yours. He's already askin' you to scratch 'is ears.'

The horse was doing exactly that, rubbing his head against Ike. He responded, not only scratching his ears but petting him and talking to him. 'I guess Surprise fits him better'n anything I can think of at the moment,' he said.

As if time were suddenly being wasted unacceptably, Ross said, 'Well, get your gear on to your reg'lar horse. We gotta get to work. There's a lot o' cows to get moved afore dark.'

No matter how impatient the crew suddenly was, Ike took time to give the gelding a good rub-down and a generous bait of oats before they rode out. That meant he had to lope a ways to catch up, but he didn't mind.

CHAPTER 6

Unease crept through Ike's mind. He had no idea of its source. He couldn't identify anything that should pose a threat. The feeling was odd, out of place, baseless. But it was there.

It was there as he saddled up Morgenstern shortly after sunrise. The mare was one of the ranch horses that was part of his string. He didn't really know why he named her that. He knew the name meant 'Morning Star' in German, and he thought it was fitting, especially with the white star in the middle of her forehead. His unease seemed to be transmitted to her through his attitude or his touch or the tone of his voice. She began to mirror it. She was jittery. Her steps didn't have their usual spring. She just wasn't quite herself.

He was paired with Stuttering Leroy for the day. He enjoyed working with him. He wasn't sure whether it was because he didn't talk much, so their work wasn't interrupted constantly by chatter, or just that he did his job so effortlessly and efficiently. He was just a good hand to work with. He felt relaxed whenever he and Leroy were paired together.

That wasn't the case today, however. The sense of pending problems plagued Ike throughout the day. They had previously moved a large bunch of heifers to a broad valley less than a mile from ranch headquarters, where they would be more accessible for calving. Now the wisdom of that move demonstrated itself as the first-year heifers began to calve in earnest.

Morgenstern seemed able to spot a heifer having trouble even before Ike did, and was already moving toward her when he identified the one with difficulty giving birth. Even as they moved toward her, though, both man and horse kept looking around, as if expecting something threatening to appear, something that had nothing to do with cattle or calving.

When a calf was born, on its feet and nursing, there was none of the usual sense of satisfaction. In the very air hung an expectant, 'Yeah, but now what?' that was never answered.

The day wore on with nothing out of the ordinary emerging. Still the feeling remained. In late afternoon Al Reynolds and Kid Nelson showed up to take the night shift and they were relieved of duty. It was time to head back and put their horses up. Tomorrow they'd ride different mounts, to allow today's horses to rest. Even as they headed toward the ranch, that unease niggled away in the back of Ike's mind.

Ike was tired. He and Leroy MacAllister were within half a mile of the U-V-Cross ranch yard. The heifers they were assigned to tend during calving were doing well. Now that Al and Kid were there to replace them for the night, they could relax for a while. Then they would return the favor just after daybreak. There was simply no reason for the unease that plagued him.

Both he and Leroy looked forward to a hot meal and bed. Calving, especially calving first-calf heifers, was strenuous, demanding, exhausting work. Often a cow's first calf needed pulling, or she needed to be tied to something so she'd let the calf nurse the first time. There was an occasional prolapse to deal with. There were any of a dozen other problems that could – and often did – arise. After more than a week of the demanding schedule, the men and their horses were bone-weary.

Then he saw it. It was just a minor movement in the brush. There was no reason it should alarm anyone. Things moved in the brush all the time, especially as evening approached. That was especially true during calving, when there was an abundance of afterbirth and the like that made easy and bountiful meals for coyotes and lesser scavengers.

Ike could not have explained why the movement in the brush shot alarms through his mind. He didn't take time to wonder. Too many near-fatal incidents had honed his instincts to a razor's edge, and he never doubted them.

The instant he spotted the movement he yelled, 'Look out!' and dived from the saddle. Even as he did he felt a burning sensation sear across the left side of his neck. The sound of a rifle shot reached his ears an instant later.

To his credit, Leroy's reactions were much quicker than his ability to say anything. An instant behind Ike he left the saddle in a long dive, tucked his shoulder and rolled.

Ike wasn't aware of pulling his rifle from its scabbard on the saddle as he dived, but it was in his hands. With an instinct honed by long training, he hit the ground and flopped into a prone firing position. He fired four swift rounds into the brush where he had spotted the movement.

Crashing in the brush indicated their attacker had taken flight. He was aware, however, that there might be more than one.

He leaped to his feet and ran a zig-zag path toward the cover of brush and trees, heading for a spot about thirty yards to the left of where the shot had come from. Out of a corner of his eye he saw Leroy doing the same thing, heading for a spot that would put him into the cover fifty yards to Ike's right.

He reached the cover of the timber and crouched, listening. In the distance he could hear the running hoof-beats of a single horse. There was no other sound. Moving silently he worked his way to where he thought the shot had originated. He found the spot quickly, seeing the trampled brush easily, even in the fading light.

'Looks like there was just one, and he lit out.'

The words startled Ike nearly as much as the sneak attack had done. He stared in disbelief at Leroy, who had moved silently up beside him. Instead of the dozen questions that rattled around in his mind, Ike said, 'Any idea who it was?'

Leroy shrugged. 'Devlin, most likely.'

'Why would Devlin try to bushwhack me?'

'You whipped him.'

'People don't just lay in wait and shoot someone because they got whipped in a fight!'

'Devlin would.'

Ike couldn't resist the question that crowded even the danger out of his mind. 'Why ain't you stutterin'?' he demanded.

Leroy shrugged. 'W-w-wasn't thinkin' about it.'

'Who's shootin' out here?' a call came from the distance. Ike recognized Ross Endicott's voice.

'We're in the timber over here, Ross,' Ike called back.

'You hurt?'

'We're OK.'

'Who's shootin'?' The sound of the voice indicated Ross was riding swiftly toward them.

'Don't know,' Ike responded. 'Someone took a shot at me from the brush.'

'Someone tried to bushwhack you?'

'Yeah. Grazed my neck.'

'Devlin?' Ross guessed.

'That's Leroy's guess, anyway,' Ike answered.

As he and Leroy walked out into the open, Ross and Ivle Andersen drew rein beside them. Al surveyed the blood already soaking Ike's collar and shirt. 'Came mighty close,' he observed.

'I saw the brush move and dived off my horse,' Ike explained. 'He probably wouldn't have missed otherwise.'

His jaw set, his eyes narrowed, Ross said, 'He'll try again, you know.'

'Yeah,' Ike agreed.

'Well, let's get back to the place. Clarissa will take a look at that neck an' get you bandaged up. She's better'n most doctors. The problem is Devlin. He'll be back, sooner or later.'

Ike knew it was only a matter of when and where.

CHAPTER 7

Days turned into weeks with the slow turning of that inexorable millwheel of time that grinds us all down, puts lines in our faces and aches in our joints. Ike was harnessing a team one morning when a familiar voice asked, 'What'cha doin' today, Mr Ike?'

He smiled at Billy, enjoying the endless enthusiasm that always animated his voice. 'Ross says I need to cultivate the corn today.'

'What's cullyvate?'

'That's when we get rid o' the weeds growin' between the rows.'

'How do you do that?'

'With the go-devil.'

'With what devil? I thought the devil was somethin' bad.'

Ike smiled. 'Well, the Devil is bad. But a go-devil is just the name of a machine the horses or mules pull. It goes along and turns up the ground between the rows of corn.'

Billy visibly pondered the information. 'Then a go-devil is a thing what cullyvates, an' not a real devil?'

43

'Exactly right!' Ike confirmed.

'Can I ride along?'

Ike thought it over for a minute. 'Yeah, I think that'd be OK, if it's OK with your ma.'

'Aw, she won't care. She don't worry 'bout me none when I'm with you.'

Ike smiled. 'Well, I'm glad she feels that way. But you need to ask her anyway. You can go do that while I get the team harnessed up.'

Billy started to turn from the barn, then stopped. Turning back to Ike he said, 'You won't go startin' without me, will ya?'

'No, I'll wait for ya.'

He finished harnessing the team of mules and led them to where the cultivator waited amid a rapidly growing patch of Russian thistles. He hitched them to the implement, then sat down on the crossbar waiting.

When Billy failed to appear, he walked to the house. He was just stepping up on to the porch when Minerva opened the door and stepped out. He removed his hat instantly. 'Ma'am. I told Billy I wouldn't start cultivatin' till he asked you if he could ride along.'

Minerva smiled broadly, glancing over her shoulder. 'He's been giving me an endless string of reasons he really needs to do that,' she said. 'He's taken quite a liking to you.'

'He's a fine boy. He asks more questions than I can answer, but he remembers what he's told. He never has to ask the same one twice.'

'Will he be any trouble? There's not much place for him to ride, is there?'

'Not much,' he acknowledged, 'but he'll get tired afore long. He can either stand on the main bar right beside me, or sit on my lap, till he's had his fill of it.'

From behind Minerva an eager voice piped up, 'See, Ma? I said there was plenty o' room. I wanta help cullyvate with the go-devil.'

'Oh, very well,' she assented. 'But you watch out for rattlesnakes if you walk back from the field.'

'I allays do,' Billy responded, the insult to his manly pride heavy in his voice. ''Sides, Maverick allays comes with me ever'where. He don't let no rattlers get close.'

'I've noticed that dog isn't ever very far from him when he's outside,' Ike agreed.

She nodded. 'I'd be afraid to let him play outside without the dog.'

A few steps from the house Billy's hand slipped into Ike's. A warm glow settled through him as he watched the lad try to imitate his walk.

As Ike settled into the seat of the cultivator, Billy climbed up beside him. He found a good spot to stand, holding on to Ike's shirt for balance. When he stopped the team at the gate, Billy bailed off the machine before Ike had hardly moved. He was running almost before his feet hit the ground. 'I'll get the gate,' he hollered.

Ike sat still, watching with amusement as the boy struggled in vain to push the gate post enough to loosen the tension on the wire loop that held it shut. When he had let him struggle a reasonable amount of time, he wrapped the lines around one of the levers and climbed down.

'Maybe I oughta help you just a little bit,' he offered.

'I just need somethin' to stand on,' Billy apologized. 'I

45

can't reach it good enough to use my weight to 'vantage.'

'Yeah, I think that's all you need, all right. It won't be long before you're tall enough to put a shoulder on the post, though.'

As he swung the gate open, Billy hollered, 'I'll drive 'em through the gate.'

He scampered on to the cultivator, climbed into the seat and unwrapped the lines. 'Geyupp!' he yelled.

More because the gate was open than from his imperious command, the mules moved through the gate and stopped. It wasn't until they were fully stopped that Billy thought to holler, 'Whoa there!'

He sat there in the seat like a king on his throne while Ike closed the gate behind them. As Ike climbed back up on to the cultivator, he asked, 'You want me to drive 'em for a while?'

Stifling the urge to laugh aloud, Ike replied with mock seriousness, 'Well, maybe I'd oughta do the drivin'. If Ross sees you doin' it, he might decide the place don't need me. Then I'd be out've a job. You can help me watch, though, to make sure we set the shovels deep enough to get rid of the weeds without turnin' up any o' the corn.'

'OK! You go right ahead an' drive then, and I'll watch to make sure you do it right.'

He watched diligently as the cultivator did its job for the better part of fifteen minutes. For the next hour after that, he kept up an incessant stream of questions.

As they approached the nearest point of their second round to the gate, Billy said, 'I 'spect them mules are gettin' a little tired o' pullin' all the extra weight, with me ridin' on here.'

Ike nodded. 'They are lookin' a little weary,' he agreed. 'It might be a good idea to see if your ma's needin' a little help in the house, anyway.'

He pulled the team to a stop and Billy clambered off, running for the gate. Twice a foot caught in the soft, fresh soil and he fell headlong. Each time he sprang to his feet, seeming to already be running again by the time he was upright. 'I'll just climb through the gate 'stead o' openin' it,' he called over his shoulder.

Ike watched until he spotted the black and white dog rise from where he had been waiting. He trotted along, keeping pace with the youngster as he ran toward the house.

'That boy'd wear out a good man with all that energy,' he muttered. 'I don't know how his ma keeps up.'

CHAPTER 8

'Hi, Mr Ike.'

'Well, good mornin', Fred.'

Billy's head jerked up to focus squarely on Ike. 'My name ain't Fred!'

'Oh! Sorry. Good mornin', George.'

Billy's fists doubled and went to his waist. 'You know that ain't my name, neither.'

'Oh! Well remind me. What is your name, again?'

'You know!'

'Ah! Well, that's sort of an odd name, but if you say so. Good mornin', Mr You Know.'

Billy stamped a foot in the loose straw of the barn floor. He glared at Ike's back. Ike was busily harnessing one of the Percherons so he couldn't see his expression. Stamping the floor did even less good than it might have done if it had made any sound. 'Mr Ike, why do you allays gotta tease me so much?'

Ike finally turned to look at the youngster. 'Oh, maybe just because I like you.'

'I don't get why you can't like me without teasin' me alla time.'

Ike grinned. 'Well I guess I could do this instead.'

He whirled and picked the boy up. Hugging him close he thrust his face just below the lad's left ear and began whiskering the side of his neck. Billy squirmed and giggled as if trying his best to get away, but his arms betrayed him. They reached around Ike's shoulders, hugging him tightly.

When he set him back down, Billy feigned anger. 'Just you wait till I grow up some! Then you ain't gonna be able to do stuff like that to me.'

Ike lifted the boy's cap, ruffled his hair, then slapped the cap back on so it was down over his eyes. Instead of responding, Billy just moved it up on to his head and asked, 'Whatcha doin' today, Mr Ike?'

'Fixin' fence.'

'Is it busted?'

'No, I don't think it's busted anyplace. But it needs checking and tightening up good. The corn's gettin' tall enough all those big green leaves look awful good to the cows, so they'll be tryin' their best to figure out a way to get to it.'

'It sure is plumb dry again this year, ain't it?'

'Yeah, it is, Billy. If it wasn't for that crick, we wouldn't have any corn at all. I don't think it would've even sprouted without irrigatin' it.'

'It looks plumb good to me. 'Specially what you'n me planted. It seems to me that them rows look a mite taller than the rest of it.'

Ike turned back to the harness to hide his grin. 'I'm

sure that makes a difference all right.'

'Can I go with ya today? I ain't never learned how to fix fence. High time I did, since I'm gettin' older.'

'Well, if that's all right with your ma, I guess so.'

'Aw, she won't care, as long as I'm with you.'

'You need to ask her anyway.'

'Oh, OK.'

He started to leave the barn then turned back. 'Mr Ike, don't you like my ma?'

Ike stopped what he was doing and turned. 'Well yeah. Of course. Why would you ask that?'

'Well, you don't never tease her. You said you tease me all the time 'cause you like me. An' you tease Minnie some, if she happens to be outside with me, so I guess you like her OK, too. So if you like my ma, why don't you never tease her?'

Ike found himself stammering. 'Well, I . . . If I did . . . It . . . Well, I just don't want her gettin' any wrong ideas about me.'

'What wrong ideas would she get from you teasin' her?'

Ike scratched a sudden itch on the back of his neck. 'Well, that's kinda hard to explain.'

'Why?'

'Now that's Minnie's question.'

'What?'

'No. Not what. Why?'

'Huh?'

'Minnie's the one that always asks "Why?" to everything. You can't be using her question.'

Billy frowned in total confusion. 'Just 'cause she uses a word don't mean I can't use it no more.'

'Why not?'

'Ha! See there! You used it.'

'Well so I did. So I guess you can use it once in a while too. Just not as often as Minnie does.'

'Yeah, she uses it every time anyone says anything. 'Why? Why? Why?' She just plumb wears me out with "Why?" '

'Well if you're gonna go with me to fix fence, you better go ask your ma.'

'OK. But you ain't answered my question yet.'

'Which one? It seems to me there were half a dozen at least. Which one didn't I answer?'

'I asked if you like my ma.'

'Oh. That one. I thought I answered it. I said yes.'

'But you didn't really say "Yes", you said something that sounded sorta like yes, but not really. Ma says you allays eat in the cook shack with the rest o' the crew 'cause you ain't never asked to eat supper with us. So do you like my ma, or don't ya?'

Ike took a deep breath. 'OK, Billy. Yes. I like your ma. I think she's a mighty fine woman. In fact, I think she's just about the finest woman I've ever known. Now if you're going to go with me, get to the house and see if it's all right.'

With a big grin betraying he had just heard something he really wanted to hear, Billy wheeled and headed for the house. At a dead run, of course. As always.

They were two hours into fixing fence when Billy leaned against a wheel of the buckboard that carried the posts, wire, wire stretcher, staples, and other supplies. 'Mr Ike, don't you think maybe them horses is gettin' to need a drink? It's awful hot out here, an' we done drank most all the water in your canteen. Maybe we oughta take them horses back to the yard so they can have a drink too.'

Ike eyed the boy carefully, noting his sweat-streaked shirt and slumped shoulders. He nodded. 'Yeah, those horses do look like they're a little hot and tired. Hop up on the buckboard and we'll take 'em to get a drink and a bait of oats.'

Billy clambered up on to the seat of the buckboard. He used a sleeve to wipe the sweat from his face. 'Boy, this fencin' sure is hard work. I bet that's why most o' the guys hate doin' it.'

'It sure ain't a cowpoke's favorite job, that's for sure,' Ike agreed.

'How come you like doin' it?'

'Now I don't remember sayin' I liked any part o' fencin'.'

'You don't like doin' it?'

'Nope.'

'Then how come you do it?'

' 'Cause it needs doin'.'

'Yeah, but them there other guys could do it, too.'

'They take their turn.'

'Huh! Ma says you're the only one that does your fair share of it an' more.'

'Well, that's just part o' bein' a man, Billy. You do the work that needs doin', do a little more than what you have to, do the very best job you can all the time, and don't worry about what the other guy is doin' or not doin'.'

It didn't take any argument to convince Billy he ought to go see if his ma needed some help in the house instead of going back to the fencing.

CHAPTER 9

'Mr Murdo.'

Ike turned toward the voice. He found himself face to face with Minerva Vogel. He swept his hat off instantly. 'Yes, ma'am?'

Irritation furrowed her brow fleetingly. 'Please don't call me that,' she said. 'My name's Minerva.'

'Yes ma— uh, Minerva.'

She laughed lightly at his discomfiture. He recovered quickly. 'Of course, if I do that, then you have to drop the "Mr".'

Dimples appeared at the corners of her mouth. 'Oh. You would prefer me to call you Murdo?'

He grinned. 'Well, that'd be better'n Isaiah, I guess.'

'I could call you Enos, but you already told me that name was off limits when you finally told me what it was.'

'Way off limits,' he agreed. 'Ike would be just fine, though.'

'Fair enough, Ike,' she said. 'I wonder if I could commandeer your services today?'

'For what, Ma— uh, Minerva?'

54

'I promised the children I would take them on a picnic up at the falls. You've seen the falls, I presume.'

'Yes . . . uh . . . yes, I've been up there. It's a beautiful spot.'

She nodded. 'It's especially beautiful this time of year. The wild flowers up there are absolutely magnificent. We used to picnic up there a lot, before . . . when Kirk was . . . with us. Ross and Clarissa are pretty protective. They don't like it if we go up there without an escort. Since you seem to have such a good rapport with Billy, I wondered if you would see fit to provide us that escort today.'

Something swelled from within him that Ike was at a loss to understand, but there was no denying its intensity. He fought to keep any huskiness out of his voice. 'Why, I'd be just plumb happy to,' he said, 'especially if it includes a picnic dinner.'

She smiled. 'Would fried chicken and potato salad provide sufficient enticement?'

'To be real honest, hardtack and jerky would be more enticement than you'd need, as long as it includes your company. I 'spect I probably oughta check with Ross, though. I don't know what he's plannin' on me doin' today.'

A whisper of irritation flitted across her face before she said, 'By all means. I do try never to supersede my foreman's orders.'

She gently but unmistakably stressed the word 'my' as she said it.

He grinned, but did not comment. Instead he said, 'I'll let 'im know. How soon will you be wantin' to leave?'

'In about an hour, if that'll work for you.'

'Sure. Do you want the buggy hitched up, or will we all be ridin'?'

'Will the buggy make it up there all right?'

'Oh yeah, I think so. If we swing a ways to the west and then come up over that low ridge, it's pretty smooth all the way, I think.'

She pursed her lips thoughtfully. 'Well, Billy could ride his pony just fine, but I don't know if Minnie would ride double very well for that long. Maybe we should use the buggy.'

'I'll get a team hitched up an' be ready,' he promised.

He found Ross discussing a repair of the cultivator with Al Reynolds and Morris Andersen. Morris was known simply as 'Dane' to the crew. His hulking bulk and over-sized arms made the foreman look small beside him. Dane's son, Ivle, stood at his father's side. Already nearly as tall as his father, he had arms and shoulders that betrayed how much he was already working at the trade at which his father was so adept. Ivle loved to demonstrate that he could lift his father's anvil, carry it in a circle and put it back on the stump where it normally rested.

Ike waited for a lull in the conversation. Ross turned to him, eyebrows raised interrogatively. 'Minerva asked me if I could escort her an' the kids up to the falls for a picnic today,' he said. 'Will that be any problem?'

Ross looked at him appraisingly, as if seeing him differently than he had done before. He almost smiled. 'It wouldn't make a whole lot o' difference if it was, would it? She's the boss.'

'Yeah, but you're the foreman.'

'The foreman's always a straw-boss,' Ross stated. 'Make

no mistake about it, that little lady runs this place. If she says "Jump", I dang well ask "How high?" when I'm already on the way up.'

Ike grinned and turned toward the barn to get the team hitched to the buggy. It was almost exactly an hour when he pulled up in front of the house. Billy came bounding out the door. 'Hey, Mr Ike! You gonna drive us up to the falls?'

'Yup.'

'Good! Can I ride Dusty an' just follow along?'

Ike glanced toward the house. 'Well, now, you'd have to ask your ma about that. It'd be easier if you just rode in the buggy with us.'

Billy tried to muster up some disappointment but wasn't very successful. 'Aw, all right. I get to ride up front with you an' Ma, though.'

'Well, who'd look after Minnie, then? It seems to me she'd be safer if she had a big strong brother sittin' beside her to look after her.'

Billy stared at him thoughtfully. 'Well, I guess maybe I could do that, all right. She's a-gonna pester me with questions somethin' awful the whole way, though. Then every time I answer one of her questions, she's gonna say, "Why?" '

Ike grinned. 'Well, maybe we could just call her "Minnie Why".'

'Her name's Minnie Mae,' Billy responded, obviously missing the joke.

'Well, then, how about "Minnie Mae Ask Why?" '

Billy frowned at him. 'That don't make no sense.'

'When she gets a little older Minnie Mae Not Ask Why So Much.'

'That still don't make sense.'

Ike lifted Billy's hat and ruffled his hair affectionately, then dropped the hat back on his head. 'Well, that's OK. Lots o' things don't make sense. Is your ma about ready?'

Billy adjusted his hat. 'I'll go check,' he offered. The last half of the sentence was said over his shoulder as he dashed back into the house.

Ike wrapped the reins around the brake lever and climbed down. He just reached the front door as it opened. He and Minerva nearly ran into each other. 'Oh!' she said, as she stepped back.

'Sorry,' Ike offered instantly. 'I didn't mean to startle you. Can I carry somethin'?'

He was surprised at the blush that colored her face instantly as she stepped back. She recovered immediately. 'Yes, if you would. The basket and things are on the table.'

As she lifted Minnie into the back seat of the buggy, Ike carried out the stack of things she had placed on the table. The smell of fried chicken wafted up from within the basket. By the time he had things loaded the rest were already settled into their seats.

He climbed into the seat beside Minerva and clucked to the team. They left the yard at an easy walk.

The June sun was warm, but it was not solely responsible for the glow that spread through Ike as they drove. They chatted about several things on the ranch, and even got into a discussion of politics. 'Your old commander is the president now,' she observed.

He looked at her in surprise, then nodded. 'He'll do all right. He's a good man. He'll make a lot o' enemies, I 'spect. He hates that the government is mostly run by people that get the position just by knowin' someone. He'll make some of his friends mad, even, because he won't do that. But he'll do what's right. How'd you know he was my commander in the war?'

'Ross told me. Was it really bad? The war, I mean.'

'It was worse'n bad. War always is.'

'You don't wear a gun. Is the war the reason?'

He pondered the question a long moment. Finally he said, 'If a man ain't wearin' a gun, he's less likely to depend on it. Most things can be settled without one.'

'So you won't use one?'

He shook his head. 'I didn't say that. I just said I'd rather settle things without usin' one, if I can. A man oughtn't ever be too quick to take up a gun, nor too reluctant, on the other hand, if there's a reason.'

'It could be pretty hard to know the right time then, couldn't it?'

'Sometimes,' he admitted.

They arrived at the falls after a delightful hour's drive. He managed to steer the team skillfully around nearly every rock or ditch that would have bounced the conveyance around. Billy and Minnie both kept up an endless flurry of questions about everything they saw. Ike and Minerva more or less took turns answering.

They found themselves together mouthing the word 'Why?' just as soon as they answered one of Minnie's questions. When they realized they were both doing so simultaneously, Minerva giggled, her eyes dancing. After that it became a game they both enjoyed. Once, as they mouthed the word, no sound came from Minnie. Both of them whirled at the same time to see what was wrong.

59

They caught Billy with his hand over her mouth.

'Billy!' Minerva expostulated.

Looking chagrined, Billy said, 'Aw, I just get plumb frazzled listenin' to her say "Why?" every time anyone says somethin'.'

'She'll outgrow it pretty soon,' Ike assured him. 'I'm bettin' you said the word just as much when you were that age.'

'I don't remember stuff that long ago, from before I got old,' Billy disclaimed. Then he frowned because both Ike and his mother found that hilarious.

When they arrived both children ran to the creek at once. They stood in total fascination watching the water tumble down over a small cliff into a large pool flanked by boulders. At the lower end of the pool the water danced merrily over rocks and gravel as it made its way downward.

'Wow!' Billy marveled. 'I betcha there's trout in there.'

'You want to catch one?' Ike asked.

'Sure! How?'

From the back of the buggy Ike brought out a fishing pole made of a six-foot stick and a length of line with a hook on the end. 'Let's see if we can find a worm,' he said.

He turned over a large rock and picked up a large pinkish-brown worm. He put it on the hook and told Billy, 'Come over along the edge, right about here. Stay down real low and crawl toward the edge. Now just reach the pole way out in front of you and drop the worm in the water, right along the edge. Just let the current carry it along. Stay back out of sight, because if a trout sees you it won't bite on anything.'

Helping the lad hold on to the pole he dangled the

worm into the water. It had carried less than six feet along when it jerked violently. Billy gasped. If Ike hadn't been hanging on too, it would have jerked pole and all away from the youngster. Chuckling, Ike helped him lift the flopping fish out of the water and away from the bank.

'Wow!' Billy said again. 'That's a big ol' fish! Is that a trout?'

'That's a rainbow trout, all right,' Ike assured him. 'Should we cook it?'

'Yeah!'

'I wanna catch a fish too,' Minnie demanded.

'OK,' Ike agreed. 'Let's find another worm.'

He had to turn over three rocks before they found a nice worm beneath one. He coaxed her into picking it up and handing it to him by threat of not letting her fish if she didn't. She finally did, holding it out at arm's length, while Minerva giggled at the scene. He baited the hook and repeated the process just a little way downstream from where Billy had caught his fish. It took no longer than it had with Billy's before another nice trout took the bait. Minnie squealed as the pole jerked, then squealed again as he helped her haul it out on to the bank.

Her first words were, 'Is mine bigger than Billy's?'

'They're both really big fish,' Ike evaded. 'Let's make a fire and cook 'em.'

He built a small fire, then cleaned the fish, washing them in the stream. Then he buried them in the ashes of the fire to let them bake.

Minerva spread a large blanket on a clear patch of grass, surrounded by a profusion of wild flowers of every imaginable size, shape and color. Ike showed the children

61

how to peel the cooked skin, scales intact, off of the fish, then lift the meat gently off of the bones with their forks, leaving the entire skeleton of the fish intact and the meat free from bones. Minerva apportioned it out on the four plates to supplement what was already a surfeit of food she had packed in the basket. They ate what Ike thought was the most delicious and delightful meal he had ever eaten. He and Minerva sat there talking when they were finished, while the children romped and played.

Abruptly Ike said, 'Uh oh!' He rose to his feet.

'What is it?' Minerva demanded.

'Move slow-like to the buggy and stay real quiet,' he said softly.

Moving slowly he backed to the buggy. Reaching under the seat he extracted a 44.40 carbine. He called out to the children. 'Billy, Minnie, come back to the buggy.'

Both children stopped and stared at him. Ike called again. 'Billy, get Minnie by the hand, and the two of you walk this way. Do not run. Just walk. Now.'

He walked slowly toward them as they stood staring at him.

Minerva had moved to the buggy. She stood against a front wheel, confusion furrowing her brow. Looking in the direction Ike kept watching, she suddenly saw the bushes along the creek bank moving. She drew in a sharp breath. Her hand went to her mouth. She visibly fought the urge to run to her children.

'Hurry up and do as I say, Billy,' Ike urged.

This time it was Billy who said, 'Why?'

Minerva's eyes were frozen on the spot where the bushes continued to move. It was obvious something was approaching the children. Ike was too far away from them! If it were a wolf or a bear or a mountain lion, it could reach the children well before he could.

Hands to her mouth, she resisted the effort to scream.

Without raising his voice Ike said, 'There's a bear in the bushes between you and the crick. I don't think it'll bother you if you don't run. If you start to run, it may think you're food and come after you. So do not run. Just walk to the buggy. Hold on to Minnie.'

Billy's head swiveled around for a moment, trying to grasp what he was being told. He abruptly understood the danger of the moment. His eyes grew to the size of saucers. He grabbed his sister's hand and said, 'C'mon, Minnie.'

He lunged forward, nearly dragging Minnie off her feet. 'Slow down!' Ike commanded. 'Just walk!'

With obvious effort, Billy did so, watching back over his shoulder more than he watched where they were going. As they walked toward the buggy Ike kept walking toward them. When he was between them and the bear he began to walk backward, keeping himself between them and the danger that threatened. They were halfway to the buggy when the bear poked its head out of the brush, watching them intently.

The large black bear sow lifted her snout, sniffing the air. She swung her massive head back and forth several times, testing the scents in the air. She opened her mouth wide and reared up, standing on her hind legs. Behind him Ike heard a small chirp emit unbidden from Minerva's throat as the huge animal did so.

'Go on to the buggy. Just keep moving,' Ike said. 'Don't

run. We're fine. She's just looking things over. She wants to know we ain't a threat to her or an easy lunch, either one. As long as her cubs don't come waltzin' along, she ain't gonna bother us.'

The horses were very obviously not as certain of that as Ike sounded. They were prancing nervously, clearly wanting to be somewhere else, tugging against the set brake of the buggy then backing up against the single trees.

The bear lowered herself to all fours again and appeared to lose all interest in them. She turned back into the brush and disappeared. They heard her for several minutes as she made her way down the creek.

Ike breathed a deep sigh of relief.

Minerva hustled her children into the buggy and stood looking at Ike. He spent several minutes calming the team. Wanting to appear more at ease than he was, Ike slid the rifle back under the seat. 'I don't think she'll come back, but I 'spect we'd just as well gather stuff up and head back home,' he suggested.

Minerva glanced once more in the direction in which the bear had departed then back at Ike. She nodded her head. Together they gathered their things, folded up the blanket, and loaded it all into the buggy. The horses were all too happy to be on the move. They headed for home as unerringly as a homing pigeon might have.

It made far too abrupt a finish to a day that Ike didn't want to ever end.

At the house he wrapped the lines around the brake handle and climbed down. He lifted each of the children out and set them on the ground. He held up a hand to

Minerva. Instead of just taking his hand, she held out both arms. He more than gladly took the hint. Gripping her at the waist with two hands, he hoisted her out of the buggy and set her on the ground in front of him. She stayed there a long moment, hands on his arms, looking up at him. The lump in his throat prevented him from saying anything.

'Thank you so much, Ike,' she said. 'I haven't enjoyed a day that much in a very long time. Even when the bear came along, I felt perfectly safe with you.'

Ike surprised himself by saying, 'I'd be plumb proud to take you anywhere, anytime. You just say the word.'

Her dancing eyes and the flush that suffused her cheeks provided all the answer he needed. He lay awake a long time that night, remembering those eyes and that smile.

CHAPTER 10

'We've been blind-sided!'

Ike frowned at the fury lines etched in the foreman's face.

'What happened?'

'The crick's dry.'

'What?!'

'The crick's dry. I sent Ivle out to set the feed pipes to water the corn, an' she's plumb dry.'

'How could it just dry up?'

'It couldn't. Not by itself. Git your horse an' mine saddled up. You'n me are gonna check it out. I'll let the boss lady know.'

At a loss for words, Ike complied. In remarkably short order he led his horse and the foreman's to the house. He ground-tied both of them and stepped up on the porch where the other two already stood. Minerva moved over close to him as he did so. She put a hand on his arm, but continued to talk to her foreman. The action was not lost on Ross, but he said nothing.

'What will you do if Kruger's diverted it or dammed it

up or something?'

Ross glanced at Ike then looked back at his boss. 'We'll just have to see what he's got to say about it.'

Minerva's eyes darted back and forth between Ike and Ross. 'He won't . . . I mean, it's not. . . . You don't think he'll just try to take all the water, do you? I mean, I do have the letter.'

Ike frowned. 'What letter?'

She looked into his eyes. 'When we first started building the place, we had an agreement with Kruger. Each of us is entitled to half the water from the creek. Kirk asked him to send him a letter agreeing to that, and he did. I still have the letter.'

'Would you mind if I take a look at it?' Ike asked.

The foreman's expression would have been best described as appraising. Eyebrows raised, he looked back and forth between Minerva and Ike. Whatever he saw between the two was reflected in his eyes, but his face remained expressionless. He waited until Minerva brought the letter out and Ike read it.

'Perfect. That should be all we need, if it comes to that,' Ike opined, handing the letter back to her.

'Comes to what?' Minerva demanded.

Ike scratched the back of his neck. 'Well, it shouldn't need any more than just talkin' to 'im. But if he bows his neck an' decides he wants all the water, this'll give us a legal claim to half of it.'

Minerva looked hard at him, then back at her foreman. 'Do you think he'll do that?'

Ross shrugged. 'Ain't no tellin' what Kruger's apt to do. He gets pretty high-handed now and again.'

'So what are you going to do?'

'Me'n Ike'll ride over there and have a look-see. Then we'll see what he says.'

'Then what?'

'Then we'll just go from there.'

Minerva opened her mouth twice and closed it again. Clearly she was both confused and frightened. She seemed unaware her hand was still on Ike's arm. She looked up at him. 'Do be careful,' she said. 'Please?'

He nodded, not trusting himself to respond. He and Ross mounted their horses and rode out at a brisk trot.

Three hours later they found the reason for the dry creek-bed. A huge dike of raw earth stemmed any flow that remained, just past the end of a large field of corn.

'He's gone an' planted three times as big a patch o' corn as he's ever had afore,' Ross gritted. 'It looks like he's decided he gets first claim to all the water.'

'You boys lookin' for somethin'?' a coarse voice demanded.

Three men rode up, stopping their horses a few yards away, obviously spacing themselves far enough apart to be in position of advantage in case of a confrontation.

'You got no right to dam up this crick like that,' Ross asserted. 'Half that water belongs to us.'

Big Dan Devlin grinned wickedly. 'Not if Kruger decides it's his.'

'Well, we'll have to have a talk with Kruger, then,' Ross declared.

Devlin shrugged. 'You kin try if you wanta, I guess. Ain't gonna do ya no good, though. He already told us he didn't wanta talk to the likes o' you.'

Ross's hand slid down close to the handle of his pistol. Ike swiftly sized up the situation. All three of the men bracing them wore tied-down Colts, but did not appear to him to be overly dangerous with them. Mostly they appeared to be toughs who were accustomed to bullying their way through situations without being seriously challenged.

Even so, he would be hard-pressed to pull his rifle from its scabbard quickly enough to respond if they decided to draw their weapons. He was almost certain Ross would be killed, if it came to that. Since he wore a gun and Ike didn't, Ross would be their first target.

Without saying anything, Ike hissed hard and jammed his spurs into the sides of Surprise, the horse he was riding. The big gelding lived up to his name. He lunged forward, ramming into Devlin's horse, knocking him flat. Devlin was so taken by surprise he didn't even manage to lift his foot clear of the stirrup. That foot was trapped beneath the flailing animal, taking him temporarily out of the picture.

At the same time Surprise rammed the other horse, Ike lunged from the saddle, his rifle in his hand. He grabbed the foot of the nearest man and heaved upward, toppling him from the saddle.

Over the top of the suddenly empty saddle, he leveled his rifle at the remaining opponent. Staring slack-jawed, the man made no attempt to draw his gun.

Ross made use of the sudden flurry of activity to draw his own gun. Covering the trio he said, 'You boys had best shuck them guns.'

Devlin looked back and forth between Ike and Ross, his

face purple with anger. His horse had struggled back to its feet. Devlin stood, but he limped noticeably on the leg that had been beneath it. He swore angrily, but made no move for his gun.

Ike had moved from beside the second man's horse and covered the other two men with his rifle. Both of them immediately complied with the command. Using a thumb and one finger, they lifted their pistols from the holsters and dropped them on the ground. Slowly, Devlin also complied. Careful not to get between his foreman and the trio, Ike stepped forward and removed the rifles of all three from their scabbards, dropping them in a pile.

He stepped back, keeping all three within his vision, waiting for Ross to act.

Anger etched all over his face, Ross said, 'You boys get on them horses and skedaddle. You tell Kruger he's got two days to have this dam tooken off the crick. If he doesn't, you'll be hearin' from the sheriff.'

Devlin opened his mouth to respond, then clamped it shut again. He looked daggers at Ike, all but ignoring Ross. He stepped back into the saddle.

The man that Ike had unseated did the same. Following Devlin's lead, they all galloped away.

When they had gathered the guns, Ike said, 'Now what?'

'I guess we'd best go right ahead and have a friendly visit with our neighbor, Mr Kruger.'

An hour later they sat their horses before the big ranch house on the K-K-Bar ranch. Kameron Kruger stood slightly spraddle-legged, blue eyes blazing, arms hanging from massive shoulders that were hunched slightly forward. At his feet was the pile of guns Ike and Ross had taken from his men. They didn't advertise the fact, but they had removed the cartridges from all of them.

Ross and Kruger were engaged in heated debate.

'You got three times the corn planted you've ever raised afore,' Ross stated, for the sixth or seventh time he had leveled the accusation.

Kruger shrugged. 'So what if I do? I can plant whatever I want. With this drought, folks all over the country are cryin' for feed. Corn's gonna be worth two or three times what it usually is. It's the right time to make the fields bigger.'

'But that much corn takes too much water,' Ross countered. 'You've shut off the water our corn an' our hay meadows both need.'

'As long as that crick runs through my land, I can do as I wish with it,' he asserted.

Ross shook his head. 'Not if it interferes with our half of the water,' he argued.

'You got no right to anything except what passes through my land and makes its way to yours,' Kruger insisted.

'Well, then, I guess we'll just have to let the court decide the matter.'

'Go right ahead,' Kruger blustered. 'By the time the court gets around to doin' anything it'll be past growin' season anyway.'

'We'll see about that,' Ross replied.

As they talked, Ike kept his horse positioned so he could watch the rest of the yard, making sure they were not attacked from the rear. He kept his rifle across the saddle in front of him, just in case.

As Ross turned his horse and rode out of the yard, Ike followed, but he kept the horse turned so he could continue to watch the ranch yard. As if he had been trained to do so, Surprise followed Ross, sidling along with minced steps instead of facing the direction they were going. He marveled anew at the way the animal seemed almost able to read his mind.

Once they were clear of the yard he turned and followed the foreman. Even so the hair on the back of his neck tingled until they were well out of range.

CHAPTER 11

Kameron Kruger crossed the main street of Chickasaw, Wyoming. He leaned forward slightly, head thrust even farther ahead, walking with swift purpose.

'You!' he bellowed.

Ike Murdo turned to see if he were the one being addressed. Minerva's quick intake of breath had already telegraphed her fear. The hand he still held as he had helped her step from the buggy gripped his tightly.

Ike freed his hand and stepped protectively in front of her. 'Kruger,' he acknowledged, keeping his voice even.

'I know what you're up to, and it ain't gonna work,' Kruger asserted, jabbing a finger toward Ike.

'We're up to claimin' Mrs Vogel's rights,' Ike replied.

'You're up to tryin' to sneak into town behind my back and use some legal stunt to try to keep me from usin' the water in my crick, that's what you're doin'.'

'It's not your crick,' Ike shot back. 'Half the water in that crick belongs to Mrs Vogel.'

'Not if I use it first, it don't,' Kruger insisted.

'If you use it first, you're violating your own agreement,' Ike corrected.

'There ain't no agreement. Just 'cause I let her and her husband use what I didn't need at the time don't mean I gotta keep on lettin' her use any of it. The only thing she's got any right to is what I don't use.'

'Well, we'll just see what the judge says about that.'

'It ain't gonna do you no good to go cryin' to the judge. My lawyer found out you was comin' in to talk to 'im, and he's already there.'

Minerva stepped aside, no longer willing to simply allow Ike to speak for her. 'My lawyer will also be there, Mr Kruger. The agreement is well documented.'

Kruger's already red face deepened a shade. As if it were somehow beneath his dignity to argue with a woman, he fixed his eyes on Ike and addressed him. 'You better tell that woman you work for to back off and forget about that water. She's bitin' off a whole lot more than she can chew.'

Ike's jaw tightened. 'Why don't you tell her?' he challenged. 'She's standin' right here in front of you. Ain't you man enough to talk to her yourself?'

Kruger sputtered a brief moment, then once again addressed Ike, stabbing a thick finger toward him. 'You just be sure she understands,' he ordered.

Eyes flashing, Minerva stepped right up to Kruger. Clearly surprised, he backed up a step. Minerva immediately moved forward, keeping herself directly in front of the rancher, almost against him. As he continued to back up, she continued to move forward. As she did, she spoke loudly enough to be clearly heard by those had stopped along the street to watch the confrontation. 'Mr

Kruger, if you think you can huff and puff and bluster and I'll turn around and run from you, you've got another think coming. Half of the water in Hatfield Creek is mine, and you know it. Your sneaking underhanded trick of damming up the creek is as illegal as it can be, and you are going to remove that dam whether you want to or not. If you have anything more to say you are more than free to attend our appointment with the Justice of the Peace to see if he is as impressed by your bull-headed stupidity as I am.'

Kruger continued to back up, but Minerva stayed right in his face as she spoke. As she said the last words, his heel caught the edge of the board sidewalk. He fell backward, landing heavily on his rump. Minerva placed her hands on her hips and glared at him. 'Just as I thought,' she declared, loudly enough to be clearly heard halfway down the street. 'You aren't even man enough to stand up to a woman!'

She wheeled and stalked back to the buggy, fists clenched. In spite of her anger she fully enjoyed the ripple of laughter her words had ignited at Kruger's expense. From the corner of her eye, Ike's-grin was impossible to miss.

Ike watched the rancher carefully as he lurched to his feet and brushed himself off. For a brief moment he glared at the woman who had so clearly bested him, then turned and stormed off down the street.

Half an hour later they stood in the court room. Justice of the Peace Austin Church eyed the antagonists who stood before him. Clearly uncomfortable, he shifted his corpulent body to a better position in his chair and stroked the muttonchop whiskers that bracketed his face.

'And on what do you base your claim that the Vogel ranch has rights to half the water in Hatfield Creek?' he queried Conrad Williams, the lawyer Minerva had chosen to represent her at the hearing.

Standing, Williams approached the bench. He held out a piece of paper. 'We have here a letter, penned in his own hand and signed by Kameron Kruger, acknowledging the agreement between his ranch and my client's ranch to share the waters of Hatfield Creek fifty-fifty.'

Church took the document, adjusted his glasses, and perused it carefully. He nodded, then extended it to Hubert Glass, Kruger's attorney. 'It seems to be a very clear-cut case,' he opined.

Glass seized the piece of paper and scowled at it for several minutes. He kept glancing at Kruger, who glowered from his chair. He cleared his throat. 'I, um, Your Honor, this document is not notarized. I don't believe it can be construed as a legally binding document.'

'It is in Kruger's handwriting, is it not?' the judge demanded.

Glass glanced quickly at Kruger and frowned again. 'I would not be able to ascertain that with any certainty,' he hedged.

'Then ask him!' the judge demanded.

Clearly hesitant, Glass walked over to Kruger and handed him the letter. Kruger barely glanced at it and threw it on the floor. 'That scrap o' paper don't mean a da— a blasted thing,' he huffed. 'Like you said, it ain't notarized or anything.'

Glass picked up the letter from the floor. Handing it

back to the judge he said, 'I'm afraid we have to reject this as irrelevant material, Your Honor.'

'That's not for you to decide,' the judge admonished. 'You got anything more?'

Glass cleared his throat. 'Um, I don't believe we need anything further, Your Honor. There is no dispute about the fact that Hatfield Creek flows through my client's land. That gives him first rights to its water, there being no legally binding document to the contrary.'

'Nevertheless,' the judge said, assuming his official voice, 'this court finds the letter to be a legally binding agreement between the two parties, and therefore commands and enjoins the defendant in the matter to forthwith remove all impediment to the flow of water in Hatfield Creek, and to utilize for his own purposes no more than fifty per cent of said water flow.'

He loudly smacked his desk with the wooden mallet.

'We will appeal that, Your Honor,' Glass yelled.

'Appeal and be da—' the judge caught himself in mid-word, his eyes falling on Minerva. 'Ahem. Appeal if you wish. However, inasmuch as further and lasting damage may be inflicted upon the plaintiff in this case if such impediment is not removed, I am hereby issuing an injunction decreeing that there be no such stoppage of the normal and natural flow of Hatfield Creek until such appeal is made and decided by the Circuit Judge.'

'You can't do that!' Glass yelled. 'You have to suspend your ruling pending appeal.'

'Don't lecture me on the law, Mr Glass! The court has ruled, and that's that. Court stands adjourned.'

With that he heaved his bulk to his feet and walked out

of the room.

Kruger lunged from his chair and charged out the door, leaving his attorney standing before Conrad Williams, his jaw hanging. With a measure of congeniality carefully designed to rub salt into his opponent's wounds, Williams said, 'Well, Hubert, I guess that's that. May I have the pleasure of buying you a drink?'

Glass's jaw snapped shut. His eyes flashed briefly. He took a deep breath. 'Sure, Con. You're buying, you said?'

'Of course. Tell me, do you think your client will abide by the judge's ruling?'

Glass glanced around and lowered his voice as the two lawyers walked out of the courtroom together. 'Not a chance in hell,' he muttered.

That most eloquently expressed Ike's conviction as well. As they prepared to leave town, Ike told Minerva, 'I need to go over to Western Union and send a telegram. It'll just take a few minutes.'

Minerva waited for further explanation, but he offered none. He tied the team to the hitching rail in front of the telegraph office and went inside. He was back in a quarter of an hour. 'Sorry to keep you waitin',' he apologized. 'I thought I'd ask an old friend for a little help convincin' Kruger to follow the judge's ruling.'

'You have a friend that can do that?'

Ike shrugged. 'I 'spect he can. If he sees fit, anyway.'

Again she waited for further explanation, but he offered none.

CHAPTER 12

'Are you sure that'll be enough?'

Ike's lips lifted into a tight smile, but his expression did not soften. 'It'll be just fine.'

'Handled the stuff in the war, did ya?'

'Yeah.'

Ross looked around at the assembled crew. Slim and Tubby were mounted side by side. Behind them Dane Anderson and his son hulked, both looking too big for their horses. The rest of the crew watched as the six rode out leading two well-loaded mules.

When they were half a mile from their destination, Ike said, 'No talkin' from now on. Voices carry farther than you'd think.'

Nobody questioned why Ike seemed suddenly to be in charge instead of the foreman. They just did as he said.

They rode at a walk, keeping their horses as quiet as possible. After nearly half an hour, Ike held up a hand. Motioning for the rest to stay put, he disappeared into the darkness.

The other four men on the crew looked questioningly

at Ross, squinting to see him through the gloom. He shrugged his shoulders elaborately enough for them to see, and sat his horse, waiting.

They waited in almost silence for nearly fifteen minutes. A sudden, soft flurry of sound in the distance brought them to full alert. Nothing followed.

A few minutes later Ike appeared as if by magic. 'They had a guard posted,' he said softly.

'Had?' Ross demanded.

'He's tied up with something of a headache. Let's move.'

Mounting his horse, he led the way. When he held up a hand again, they halted. When he dismounted, they did the same.

'Get the stuff and follow me,' Ike said, speaking so softly they strained to hear him.

Taking a large gunny sack from one of the mules, he started off. The others quickly lifted the rest of the mules' burdens and followed.

In minutes they stood at the edge of the dry stream bed of Hatfield Creek. Directly in front of them the large dike of fresh earth stretched into the darkness. On the upstream side of the dike water reached to within a couple feet of the top of the dam.

'Count off every five steps and dig a hole in the dike three feet deep,' Ike ordered. 'I'll set the charges.'

While the others dug, trying hard to suppress the occasional grunt that found its way through their set jaws, Ike began to string out black-wick and primer cord, laying it on the slope of the dike above where the men were digging the holes.

It was almost two hours later when Ike nodded his head with satisfaction. Primer cord extended from six places in the ground. Each cord end was wrapped around a pair of dynamite caps. Each cap was crimped on to the end of a section of black-wick. One man stood at the end of each set of fuses.

Ike spoke aloud for the first time, wanting to be sure his instructions were followed exactly. 'When I give the word, everyone light both of your fuses. Everything's double-fused, to be sure they all go off. As soon as both fuses are spittin' good, head for the horses. Move fast, but don't run. I don't want anyone fallin' down an' bustin a leg so he can't run.'

'What about the guard?' Ross demanded.

'Let him find his own dynamite,' Ike said.

Immediately he followed the wisecrack with, 'He'll be awake again by now. I'll cut him loose and send him a-runnin' with a message for Kruger. Everybody ready?'

The moon just peeking above the mountain crest pro-vided enough light for him to see a nod of affirmation from each man. 'Then let's do it!'

He struck a match and held it to the ends of the fuses he held. Other matches flared as the rest did the same.

They tried to heed his warning not to run. They really did try. They just didn't succeed very well. They walked the first few steps, but the farther they walked the faster they went. By the time they reached the horses they were all running full tilt.

Ike jerked the gag from the mouth of the guard and cut his ropes. 'If you know what's good for you, you'll run like you got wings under you,' he told the cursing guard.

81

'There's more'n a hundred pounds o' dynamite gonna go off in about a minute. You tell Kruger to be satisfied with his half o' the water or he'll think what happened tonight is just a warm-up.'

The guard looked as if he wanted to stay and argue. His eyes darted toward the dike and back to Ike twice. Spitting, sputtering fuses hissed and glowed along the length of the dike. He took off at a dead run.

So did Ike. He was in the saddle, leading the small cavalcade away from the scene when a loud explosion was followed by a series of explosions so closely spaced they blurred into one deafening roar.

The men behind Ike whooped and hollered with glee. 'Every ditch in that corn field's gonna be brim full in an hour, with all that water that's dammed up a-rushin' down,' Dane exulted.

When they rode into the ranch yard Ross said, 'I want everyone to have your rifles loaded and have plenty o' extra ammunition at hand. Slim an' Tubby, I want you in the hay mow, where you can see the whole yard out the mow door. Ivle, you get Leroy and man both doors o' the barn. Dane, you and Al keep watch from the door o' your houses. I'll do the same. Ike, you go on up to the main house an' make sure Minerva an' the kids is looked out for. The rest o' the boys can spread out in the corral, the bunkhouse, and the cook house. Make sure Ling's up an' armed too.'

It was clear the foreman expected a swift and violent response from Kruger.

He was not long in being proved right. Just as the sun was promising to make an appearance over the mountain top, the rancher galloped into the yard with eight men behind him. As they rode into the yard Ross stepped out the door of his house, rifle in hand. 'Far enough, Kruger!'

The rancher and his crew slid their horses to a stop. Kruger stood in his stirrups. 'What'dya think you're doin', Endicott?' he demanded. 'What gives you the right to ride on to my land and blow up that dam?'

'The same thing that gave you the right to build it in the first place,' Ross retorted.

Spotting one of Kruger's men slowly easing a gun from his holster, Ike yelled, 'Leave the gun where it is or you're a dead man!'

The man's eyes swiveled to Ike, standing on the front porch. His rifle, steadied against one of the posts that supported the porch roof was aimed squarely at the offending rider's middle. The man dropped the gun back into its holster, moving his hand away as if the gun butt had burned him.

As if that were a signal, the rest of the U-V-Cross crew showed themselves, every man with a rifle pointed at the group.

Kruger's face turned crimson, then purple. 'Is this the way you greet a neighbor?' he demanded.

'Is this the way a neighbor stops over to visit?' Ross retorted.

'You dynamited my dam!'

'Damn right,' Ross responded. 'You had no right to build it in the first place, and the court ordered it removed. You might say we just sorta enforced the court's order.'

'The court's got no say in what I do on my own land any

more than you do.'

'The judge thought he did. That's why he ordered the dam removed.'

'My lawyer's appealing that.'

'Fine. In the meantime, you're plumb welcome to use half the water in the crick.'

Kruger sputtered for several heartbeats. 'You just wait, Endicott. I'll have that dike back up before you can steal enough of my water to do that sorry crop o' yours any good. And this time there'll be hell to pay if you try to do anything about it.'

With one more glance around the yard, the clearly out-gunned and out-maneuvered rancher wheeled his horse and galloped out of the yard. His men followed.

They were scarcely out of the yard when Minerva was at Ike's side. 'Oh, Ike! If you hadn't seen what he was doing, that man would have shot Ross!'

Ike nodded. 'Most likely. Then everybody would've opened up and we'd have had a blood bath here.'

'I'm scared,' Minerva admitted. 'What will he do now?'

Ike took a deep breath. 'Well, he blind-sided us once, and it didn't work. He'll try again. We'll just have to wait and see, I guess.'

'I'm scared,' she said again.

He put an arm around her shoulders without really realizing what he was doing. 'Don't worry,' he soothed. 'I'm not about to let anything happen to you or your ranch, either one.'

She leaned against him, head tilted back, looking into his eyes. 'You oughta be in the house, Minerva,' Ross's voice broke into the moment.

Minerva and Ike both started as if suddenly wakened from sleep. Both looked equally uncomfortable. Ike cleared his throat. 'Uh, she, uh, didn't come out till they'd left,' he defended.

'Will they be back?' she asked her foreman.

'Not tonight. We'll have to keep a watch posted, though. Gonna be a bear tryin' to take care of a corn crop an' the cattle, an' keep the women an' kids safe, an' figger out what that danged idiot's gonna do all at the same time.'

Muttering to himself he stalked off across the yard.

'I'm scared,' Minerva said again.

Ike looked off into the distance a long moment. Finally he said, 'I need to go into town this morning. If you and the kids want to come along, it'd be a good time.'

'What are you going to do in town?'

'I need to see if I got an answer to the wire I sent.'

She looked at him with questions in her eyes, but he gave no indication that he was inclined to offer any further explanation. Finally she said, 'I do need some things. I'll have the children ready in an hour.'

CHAPTER 13

Minerva nodded off to sleep half an hour after they left the yard. As she did, she leaned farther and farther, until her head rested against Ike's shoulder. He carefully avoided moving any more than absolutely necessary, lest he wake her. It wasn't so much that he thought she needed the sleep that badly. Mostly he didn't want her to move her head from where it rested.

Halfway to town she stirred. Still half asleep, instead of sitting up straight she curled up on the buggy seat, her head resting on his leg. Gratefully he worked the kinks out of his right arm, still careful not to disturb her.

As the roof tops of Chickasaw came into sight, he reached down and gently stroked her hair that had strayed from beneath the scarf she wore, brushing it away from her ear. Her eyes flew open. She stayed as she was, rather than jerking upright as he had expected. 'We're gettin' close to town,' he said.

Suddenly recognizing the inappropriateness of her position, she sat up with a sudden, 'Oh!'

She whirled and looked over her shoulder, where Billy

86

and Minnie were curled up on the back seat, sound asleep. 'Oh!' she said again. 'I'm sorry. I must have been more tired than I thought I was.'

'That's all right. I won't tell anyone you slept with me on the way to town,' he said, keeping a perfectly straight face.

She looked startled for the barest moment, then giggled and gouged him in the ribs with her fist. 'Isaiah Murdo, you wouldn't dare!'

With an exaggerated drawl he said, 'Why that's plumb all right, Miss Minerva, ma'am, I'd just be plumb delighted to let you sleep with me any ol' time you want to.'

She giggled as she poked him in the ribs again. 'You keep a civil tongue in your head, Mr Murdo, or I'll make you walk the rest of the way to town. This is my buggy, you know.'

He grinned in response. 'I did think you'd prob'ly wanta wake up and sit up lookin' all proper when we drove into town.'

'Thank you,' she said, laying a hand on his arm. 'That was thoughtful of you. Is my hair a mess?'

She brushed at those few strands that had escaped the scarf tied securely over her hair.

'You look plumb fine. In fact, if you were any more beautiful I'd never be able to sneak a look at the road once in a while,' he assured her.

Except for the flush that brightened her face he might not have been sure she had heard him.

Both were happy their appearance had all the proper decorum as they entered Chickasaw's main street. It seemed as if everyone on the street turned to watch them intently as they passed.

'Why is everyone staring at us?' Minerva asked. The sudden nervousness caused a decided strain in her voice. 'Are you sure my hair isn't mussed or something?'

Ike frowned. 'I'm guessin' word of our little fireworks party is already the talk of the town.'

'Oh,' she replied, her relief obvious in her tone.

'Of course,' he added quickly, 'it could be that big streak o' dried drool from the corner of your mouth.'

With a quick intake of breath her hand darted to her face. Ike couldn't keep a straight face. He broke into laughter.

'Ike!' she exclaimed in a hushed tone that sounded like a subdued shout, 'you just wait until we get back outside of town! That wasn't funny!'

As he pulled the team to a halt in front of Hatfeld's mercantile store, a tall man approached. 'Would you be Ike Murdo, by any chance?'

Alarm bells erupted in Ike's mind, but stilled at once as he spotted the badge on the man's vest. 'Yes sir,' he responded, wrapping the reins around the brake handle.

'I'm United States Marshal Tom Rickenbaugh. I'm honored to meet you.'

Confusion evident on his face, Ike took the hand the marshal extended, returning the strong grip. He said, 'Pleased to meet you. Marshal, this is Minerva Vogel. I work for her.'

The marshal tipped his hat. 'Ma'am. I'm happy to meet you.'

'How do you do,' she responded as she reached across

Ike and returned his handshake as well. Ike was far more conscious of her closeness leaning across him than of the marshal's presence.

'What can I do for you, Marshal?' Ike asked.

The marshal smiled. 'Well, I'm guessin' it's more likely the other way around. What can I do for you?'

Ike frowned. 'I don't understand.'

'Is something wrong?' Minerva probed.

The marshal's smile broadened. 'Well, certainly not the way you obviously fear. No, not at all. Ma'am, I'm just a United States Marshal. When I get a telegram straight from the President of the United States asking me to ride to a place called Chickasaw, Wyoming Territory to help out a special friend of that president, I do sit up and take notice.'

Unaware of her sagging jaw, Minerva looked back and forth between the marshal and Ike several times. Ike looked more embarrassed than anything. Finally, finding her voice, Minerva said, 'Ike! You . . . You know the president?'

The marshal looked around, noting the increasing number of people on the street. They all made a strong pretense of one matter of business or another, but their common effort to work into a position to hear the conversation was laughably obvious.

'Sorta looks like the telegraph operator just might like to gossip a bit, I'm guessin',' he muttered. 'Maybe we'd oughta go over to the courthouse to talk. I'd sorta like to have the sheriff and the judge in on the conversation anyway.'

Minerva looked intently at Ike. 'Does this . . . is this . . .

any of my business? I don't want to intrude.'

'Of course it's your business. It has everything to do with you,' Ike explained.

Minerva's eyes widened as she began to add two and two together. 'Is that the wire you sent right after we went to court over the water?'

He nodded. 'Yeah. Sorry to keep you in the dark,' Ike apologized. 'It didn't seem like somethin' I oughta be talkin' about right off. I 'spect the general's awful busy. The president, I mean. I didn't know if my telegram'd even get past his secretary.'

The marshal cleared his throat. 'Like I said, I think we'd oughta go over to the courthouse to talk.'

Ike looked around, surveying the increasing numbers of people. 'Gettin' to seem like a circus is comin' to town,' he grumbled. 'We'll meet you over there.'

The marshal nodded and walked away.

As Ike slapped the reins to impel the team forward, he heard Minerva say again, 'You actually know the President of the United States?'

Ike's answer was lost in the noise of the town.

CHAPTER 14

Justice of the Peace Austin Church stroked his graying muttonchop whiskers. 'Is this an official proceeding, or are we informal here today?' he asked, looking from one person to another.

The marshal cleared his throat. 'I haven't had the pleasure of meeting you, Judge. My name's Tom Rickenbaugh. United States Marshal.'

'I'm Sheriff Edwin White, Your Honor,' offered a slender man with a moustache nearly wider than his face.

'Dang it, Ed, I know who you are. I know who you are too, Mr Murdo, inasmuch as you been in my court before. And you too, Mrs Vogel.'

'My name's Billy Vogel,' Billy announced. 'This here's my little sister, Minnie.'

'Billy! Children should be seen and not heard,' Minerva admonished.

'I was just tellin' 'im!' Billy argued.

'That's enough, young man. Now go sit down over there.'

Billy looked as if to argue, but the look in his mother's

eyes swiftly changed his mind. He took Minnie's hand and went and sat down in one of the seats.

'This ain't no formal hearing or anything,' the marshal explained, only partially hiding the smile that played at the corners of his mouth. 'We just needed a place to talk without having every busybody in town falling all over themselves to get an earful.'

'The town's a-buzzin' all right,' the judge agreed.

The marshal turned to Minerva. 'It is my understanding that you presented evidence in this court that you have a legal claim to half the water in Hatfield Creek. Is that right?'

Minerva nodded. 'My lawyer gave the judge a letter written by Kameron Kruger acknowledging an agreement that each of us has the right to half the water.'

The marshal turned to the judge. 'And on the basis of that letter, you issued a judgment enforcing that agreement?'

'I did.'

'Then what seems to be the problem?'

'Kameron Kruger,' Minerva said, before Ike could speak.

The marshal simply raised his eyebrows, waiting for a fuller answer.

Ike explained, 'Kruger thinks he can run roughshod over anyone that gets in his way. He has no intention of obeyin' any court order. His lawyer appealed the decision. The judge gave us an injunction ordering him to release our half of the water pending the appeal. He didn't have any intention of doin' it.'

'So you offered him some assistance in complying with

the court order, I understand?'

Ike hesitated. His words were careful and measured. Minerva was sure the marshal would note the hint of a smile that persisted at the corners of Ike's mouth. He said, 'It seems that a person or persons unknown did remove the dam that had been built across the crick.'

'How?'

Ike responded at once. 'Well, sir, if I were to guess, I would estimate that person or persons unknown used a hundred twenty pounds of dynamite at half a dozen locations along the dam. The evidence would indicate that pretty well did the job.'

'And was person or persons unknown accompanied or directed by any officer of the law?'

The sheriff was unable to hold his peace any longer. 'Of course they didn't have no law there. It was a bunch o' vigilantes blowin' up a legitimate thing an honest rancher had built on the crick, on his own land.'

The marshal's expression revealed that he had been in town long enough, and was good enough at his job, that he had learned exactly what he needed to know. His voice took on a hard edge. 'And you, Sheriff, as the ranking law officer in the county, did you act to enforce the court's injunction?'

'Whatd'ya mean?'

'I mean, did you, as the sheriff, whose duty it is to enforce orders issued by the court, do anything to make sure Kruger removed the dam?'

Sheriff White's moustache waggled, but no sounds issued from his mouth. The marshal kept him pinned by a flint-like glare. After several heartbeats he demanded,

'Well? Did you do your duty, Sheriff?'

White's moustache waggled a moment longer before he protested, 'I ain't sure I got jurisdiction out there.'

'You're not sure you have jurisdiction? You're not sure? You're the sheriff, and you're not sure where you do or do not have jurisdiction?'

White sputtered, 'Well, Kameron, he said his lawyer's appealin' the court order, an' I oughtn't go tryin' to do nothin' till that happens.'

'And why would you take your orders from that man, Sheriff?'

The sheriff swallowed hard a couple times. 'Well, Marshal, he ain't a good man to cross.'

The scorn in the marshal's look and tone were equally withering. 'You are a pathetic example of what no self-respecting lawman should ever be.'

Without waiting for an answer he turned to Ike. 'Isaiah Murdo, raise your right hand.'

Frowning in confusion, Ike complied. In a stern and formal voice the marshal intoned, 'Do you, Isaiah Murdo, accept the office of Deputy United States Marshal, and as such do you solemnly swear to uphold the laws of Wyoming Territory and the laws and constitution of the United States of America?'

Ike's jaw dropped. He looked at the marshal, then the judge, then at Minerva. The look in her eyes was something between pride and awe. He ignored the sheriff, whose face had suffused so darkly it was nearly purple. He swallowed hard. 'I do,' he said.

'Then here,' the marshal said, extending a badge to Ike. Ike looked at the badge a long moment, then dropped it into a pocket of his vest.

The marshal handed him a sealed envelope. 'That makes you the ranking law officer in the area. Other than me, of course. And I am formally and officially advising you, and this court, that this letter is a document directly from the President of the United States, authorizing you to act in the capacity of your office as Deputy United States Marshal to enforce the orders of this court, and to do whatever may become necessary now or in the future to prevent any unlawful withholding of the water from Hatfield Crick to which Mrs Vogel is entitled.'

'You can't do that!' the sheriff shouted, finally finding his voice.

'I just did, son,' the marshal informed the apoplectic sheriff, clearly relishing the opportunity. 'And you dang well better remember that he's got a whole lot more authority than you do, and so does anyone else that he chooses to deputize. So you just trot along now and high-tail it out to that fella that pulls all your strings, and tell 'im that he's lost this little set-to, and he'd best pull in his horns. Now git!'

His voice rose to a shout at the end. The sheriff lost no time complying, nearly falling over himself to get to the door. He paused at the door to offer a parting shot over his shoulder. 'You ain't gonna live long enough for it to matter anyway, Murdo.'

Watching him leave the marshal sent a few choice words after him, then suddenly remembered Minerva's presence. 'Uh, beggin' your pardon, ma'am. I get a bit riled up when lawmen are in the pocket o' some scoundrel.'

Minerva offered him her sweetest smile, and a voice that was so artificially cloying, and a southern drawl that was so heavily exaggerated it was comical. 'Oh don't give it another thought. Why, it was just so good of you to say the things it wouldn't be ladylike for me to say. Thank you.'

The marshal turned to Ike, his eyes twinkling. 'That's pretty much all I can do for you at the moment,' he said, as if apologizing for not bringing the army with him. 'Circuit Judge Anthony Hardwick will be here in about three weeks to hear the appeal against this court's order and injunction. Notice has been sent to Kruger's attorney, and to yours, ma'am. I'll be back for that hearing. Like I said, that's pretty much all I can do at the moment.'

'That's more than enough,' Ike said. 'I wasn't sure the general would have time to even read my telegram.'

The marshal grinned. 'He's the president, now, not the general. I sent a few inquiries after I got his telegram. Actually, I kinda kept the telegraph wires red hot for a couple days,' he admitted. 'It seemed plumb unusual, to say the least, for the President of the United States to get involved in a water dispute clear out here in Wyoming Territory. I did learn a few things. I'll just say I'd like to shake your hand one more time, and say I'm proud to know you, sir.'

Ike returned the handshake, looking embarrassed.

The marshal started to leave, then turned back to Minerva. 'Mrs Vogel, if I saw what I think I saw between the two of you, and if even half of the things I learned about this man are true, then you go ahead and grab on to him good and tight. He's one in a million.'

It was difficult to say whether she or Ike had the reddest

face as the marshal strode from the courtroom.

All Ike could think to say was, 'Thanks for the use of your courtroom, Judge.'

'It was my pleasure,' Judge Church smiled. 'This is one of those things that'll stand out in my memory for a long time.'

'Somehow I don't think Kruger's gonna be all that impressed,' Ike responded.

'There is a bit of gossip that might vindicate that feeling,' Church said.

Ike's eyebrows shot up. He said nothing, but looked at the judge quizzically, waiting for an explanation. The judge cleared his throat. 'This is street gossip, understand, but it seems likely to be true. The rumor is that Kruger has hired a fellow by the name of Nick Cadwall and two others of similar ilk to bolster his crew of hardcases.'

'Who's Nick Cadwall?'

'He is, without a doubt, the nastiest customer I have heard of in these parts. He is reputed to be faster than a rattlesnake with his gun, and totally without scruples of any kind whatever.'

'Loadin' up on gunfighters,' Ike muttered.

The judge nodded. 'That does not sound like a man that intends to obey the dictates of a court of law.'

It sounded to Ike more like he had just landed in the middle of greater jeopardy than the war itself had been.

His mind refused to dwell on it; another thought kept crowding it out. What was it the marshal had said to Minerva? 'If I saw what I think I saw between the two of you. . . .'

Did he see what Ike had been hoping for, but afraid to

dream of? Dared he dream now, when he knew a night-mare was bearing down on him that he could not walk away from?

The only thing he was totally sure of was that he couldn't do anything less than give his all to protect Minerva and her ranch. If it cost him his life, then so be it. It sounded all the time more like it might.

CHAPTER 15

The children were once again sound asleep in the back seat of the buggy. Ike and Minerva were both quiet for a long way, each lost in a private world of thought. It was Minerva who broke the silence.

'You don't like to talk about the war, do you?'

Ike looked sharply at her. He returned his eyes to the dim outline of the moonlit road ahead. He stared off into a world of images he could not rinse from his mind. It seemed to Minerva that he had chosen not to even answer, when he finally said, 'Nope.'

'Why not?'

'Some things are best forgotten.'

'Does not talking about them make them easier to forget?'

Again he was a long time answering. She held her tongue, respecting his silence, not pressing him. 'Not so far,' he said finally.

Empathy and concern gave a rich, almost throaty undertone to her voice. 'Was it really that bad?'

He met her eyes squarely for the first time since she had

brought the subject up. She tried to hide her shock at the depth of pain she saw in his eyes. She framed several things in her mind to say, but nothing found its way to audible sound.

'Yeah, it was,' he said softly.

'General Garfield – well, President Garfield – told the marshal you had saved a lot of lives by some of the things you did. Including his own.'

'Yeah. I did,' Ike admitted, as if confessing to a crime rather than making any kind of boast. 'But that meant the takin' of other lives. Those others were folks too.'

'But they were the enemy.'

His lips tightened. 'At the time, yeah, they were. But before the war started, they would have been my friends, or my neighbors. Maybe my relatives, even. But war reduces everything to just them and us. Us against the enemy. The enemy against us. Nothin' else matters. Each tryin' to kill more of the other side than gets killed on their side, so our side'll win.'

'But the president said you were very good at what you did.'

His lips drew to that thin line again. The muscles at the hinge of his jaw bulged and eased, bulged and eased. 'Yeah,' he said again. 'I guess I was. It came natural to me. Too natural. That meant I could slip around through the enemy lines and find out whatever the colonel – or the general . . . or whatever rank he was just then – needed to know. I could usually manage to keep from bein' seen. If someone did spot me, I always managed to kill him before he could give me away. But it was just one of the enemy, so it wasn't supposed to bother me that I'd killed another man. Then another. Then another. And it seemed to get easier each time. Then we'd have a big battle, and we'd see how many of them we could kill. I was good at that, too. I mostly made sure nobody got close enough to kill Garfield. I gave 'im my horse once, because his got shot out from under him. Once, I killed a sniper that was about to shoot 'im. I thought I was doin' the best job I could do for the cause of right. And I do believe our cause was right. But then I began to realize that every one of those guys that I'd killed was folks. Not bad creatures that deserved to die. Not some sort o' demons or somethin'. Folks. Just folks. Folks with family and friends back home that loved 'em, that was prayin' for God to watch over 'em and keep 'em safe and bring 'em home again. Folks just like me, doin' what they thought was right. They were prayin' to the same God I was prayin' to, askin' Him to help me kill the ones that were askin' Him to protect them. I swore once the war was over I wasn't ever goin' to set out to kill folks again. The general asked me to be in charge of his personal bodyguard after the war, and I just couldn't do it. That'd mean huntin' down folks that wanted to kill him, and hurry up and kill them first.'

Softly, after a long pause, Minerva asked, 'Do you remember the ones you killed?'

The pain in his eyes was so intense she was instantly sorry she had asked. His voice was low, but it was flat and harsh. He seemed to hunch forward over the reins he clutched more tightly than needed. 'I remember 'em. I try not to think about it. But I do, sometimes. Sometimes I can't stop thinkin' about 'em. Seein' 'em die, over and over again. Sometimes it seemed like I was seein' somebody back behind 'em too, that I couldn't see clear, because they weren't really there, so I couldn't see their features well, but I could see their grief and their pain and their loneliness. Sometimes in a dream I still see women a-standin' with a hand shadin' their eyes an' the other hand twisted in their apron, watchin' down the road because they know the war's over, and they're hopin' to see that man walkin' or ridin' toward 'em, finally comin' home at last. But he ain't ever gonna come home, because I killed him.

'Yeah, I think about 'em. I think about how good I was at what I did, and wish to God I hadn't been that good. Then I know that if I hadn't been that good, more of the guys on our side would've died instead. Or maybe the general. Or maybe a battle would've been lost. Or maybe the war, even. Then I'm glad I was that good at the same time I hate myself for bein' that good. Does that make any sense?'

'It makes perfect sense,' she said, taking his hand in hers and holding it against her face. 'Is that why you never wear a gun?'

He nodded. 'If I wear a gun, it's a whole lot more likely I'll need to use it. I got a rifle in my scabbard, or somewhere close at hand, all the time. I'd be plumb foolish not to. But that's not as obvious. The first day I was in Chickasaw I'd have had to draw against a couple guys if I'd been wearin' a gun. Since I wasn't, they contented themselves with haulin' off their friend that'd tried to whip me.'

'But what if Kameron sends some of his hands to try to kill you? He has to know by now that it's you that's keeping him from taking all the water.'

'Kameron?' Ike responded, rather than focusing on

anything else she had said.

Obviously flustered, Minerva made a dismissive motion with her hand. 'That's Kruger's first name.'

'I didn't know you were on a first-name basis with him.'

She looked uncomfortable for a brief moment, then flushed slightly. She allowed one syllable of a giggle to escape. 'I guess you could say that,' she said. 'He really tried to ... to court me, after Kirk was killed. He came over three or four times to see me. He's really quite handsome when he's all dressed up.'

Ike was torn between being glad the subject had changed from his involvement in the war, and being just as stressed to learn the ranch's nemesis had tried to court Minerva. 'He came callin' on you, huh?' he said as off-handedly as his most valiant effort allowed.

Minerva's eyes danced, clearly enjoying the discomfort the idea was causing Ike. She almost asked, 'Are you jealous?' but she managed to bite her tongue. She had no business assuming he had the feelings toward her that she was developing for him. Instead she said, 'He had a very difficult time talking about anything except what a good thing it would be for us to combine the two ranches together.'

Ike eagerly grasped at the escape from tension she was offering. 'I can almost hear him,' he asserted. His voice took on a melodramatic tone. 'Widow Vogel, ma'am, my ranch was a-wonderin' if your ranch would be interested in marryin' up with my ranch and producin' corn an' cows together? Oh, and you can come along too, as part of the deal.'

She laughed lightly. 'It wasn't quite that business-like an

approach,' she objected. Then she added, 'Well, maybe almost. It might have been less business-like if I'd been able to conceal my distaste for him a little better.'

'He is something of an arrogant sort.'

'He is an arrogant jackass, is what he is!' she surprised him by saying. 'He thinks he's entitled to whatever he wants whenever he wants it, and anybody that gets in his way needs to be stepped on like a bug. His words, by the way.'

'Not surprising he'd think that way. It is surprising he'd actually say that to a woman he was tryin' to court.'

She giggled unexpectedly. 'He wasn't exactly trying to court me then. He said that after I let him know in no uncertain terms that I had no interest in him and ordered him off my place.'

'Overstepped his bounds, did he?'

'He did.'

'Is that why he wouldn't even talk to you when we had that little discussion in the middle of the street?'

'It most certainly is. That was his typically arrogant way of announcing to me that I was not someone he cared to acknowledge as even being a person.'

She did not elaborate, and he thought better of pressing the issue. He couldn't help chuckling as he remembered the rancher backpedaling from her anger until he tripped and fell on the sidewalk, though.

It was past midnight when they pulled into the ranch yard. He carried Billy into the house and put him to bed while she did the same with Minnie. He stood at the door, facing her. He took off his hat. He cleared his throat. He studied his boots. He looked up to find her staring into his eyes. She stood almost against him. He started to speak, but the words stuck in his throat. He cleared his throat and tried again.

'Uh, Minerva. I don't want to overstep my own bounds, but I sure would be obliged if you could see your way clear to, uh, to let me court you. Formal like, I mean.'

Her eyebrows arched in mock anger. 'And aren't you afraid if that's overstepping your bounds, that I might order you off my place?'

To her surprise he bobbed his head. 'That's just exactly what I'm afraid of,' he admitted. 'And if you did, I don't think I could stand it.'

Instead of answering, she reached up both hands and pulled his head down. Their lips met. It was a quick but expressive kiss that sent his heart soaring. She stepped back, but kept her hands on both sides of his face. 'Does that answer your question?'

It was his turn to reach out and pull her to himself, returning the kiss she had given with interest. There was no questioning the enthusiasm of her response. 'We'd better get to bed,' he managed to say as he turned and walked to the buggy.

CHAPTER 16

It was almost exactly the three weeks the marshal had promised. Word was sent out to the U-V-Cross that Circuit Judge Anthony Hardwick would be in Chickasaw in three days. He would preside over cases that had been appealed or that exceeded the authority of the Justice of the Peace. The water rights case of Kruger vs. Vogel would be first on the agenda.

Ike and Minerva arrived in town well before court time. Billy and Minnie had been left in the care of Albert and Clarissa Reynolds. Clarissa had been like a second mother to the children since Kirk's death, and a true Godsend to Minerva.

Without the children present, Minerva was much more open with her feelings. As soon as they were out of sight of the yard she had scooted over next to Ike and rested her head against his shoulder. He gladly took the hint and slipped an arm around her.

Eager as he was to deal with the legal matter and move beyond it, he didn't want the trip to end. Their conversation moved easily from general things to much more personal matters. They began to openly discuss the practical things they would need to deal with in the event of their marriage.

Somewhere along the way it occurred to Ike that he hadn't actually even asked Minerva to marry him. It just seemed to be an inevitability that had grown up between them.

The more he thought about it, the more unacceptable that became. Finally he yelled, 'Whoa up there,' and pulled the team to a halt.

She looked at him questioningly. Ike twisted sideways to face her directly. He started to speak and his voice caught in his throat. He turned his head, cleared his throat, and tried again.

'I gotta ask you somethin',' he announced.

She plumbed the depths of his eyes as if trying to read there what he was about to say. 'You aren't about to tell me you have a wife and ten children back in Ohio, are you?'

He laughed aloud in spite of his nervousness. 'If I did, she'd have found me by now and drug me back by the ears,' he asserted.

She didn't respond. She just kept probing the windows of his soul.

He cleared his throat again. 'Uh, no. Nothin' like that. But I want to tell you that I love you. I love you more than life itself.'

She continued to study him intently. 'I guess it goes without saying that I love you too, Ike.'

'Well then, don't let it go without sayin',' he suggested.

'All right. I love you, Ike Murdo.'

'Minerva Vogel, will you marry me?'

107

She gasped. 'That's what you've been trying so hard to get said?'

'Well, it ain't easy to put into words!' he defended.

Her expression was so intense it was almost fierce. 'Good. I'm glad. I'm glad that's not something you could just say easily or carelessly. And yes, Ike Murdo, I will be thrilled to pieces to marry you.'

He started to say something else, but it seemed even more difficult to say anything, their lips being so involved with each other's.

After a while she pushed him gently away. 'We better get moving to town, though, my darling, or we're going to end up doing something we hadn't better be doing yet, right out here in front of God and anybody else that happens along.'

'I'd be willing to take that chance,' he teased.

She gave him that quick jab in the ribs he had come to love. 'Drive, Romeo. That waits until the preacher has his say.'

He kissed her quickly again, then snapped the reins to set the restless team moving.

The main street of Chickasaw seemed a brighter, more beautiful town than it had ever appeared before. Then he saw him.

Standing in front of Hank's Saloon, lounging carelessly against a post that supported the roof over the stoop, a man he didn't know stared at them. Though he hadn't seen him before, he knew him. He had seen the same presence in a dozen men or more. His flat eyes watched them with the same stare a cat fixes on a bird it has chosen for dinner. He rolled a match from one corner of his mouth to the other. The .45 tied low on his right hip was a perfect match for the other one, holstered at belt level, butt forward, on the other side.

Nick Cadwall, as sure as anything, Ike told himself silently.

Ignoring the man, he drove the buggy on down the street and tied up in front of the café marked with a simple sign that just said, 'EATS' in crude letters. The food, as he already knew, was far better than the artwork on the sign.

When he and Minerva had finished a hearty breakfast and two cups of coffee, they walked across to the court-house.

The appeal hearing was almost a repeat of the prior hearing before the Justice of the Peace. Circuit Judge Anthony Hardwick had in hand the court record of that proceeding, including the admission that the letter cementing the agreement to the even division of the water of Hatfield Creek was, in fact, written in Kameron Kruger's own hand.

The finding of the prior court was forthwith declared as valid and binding. Kameron Kruger hadn't bothered to attend. His attorney, Hubert Glass, appeared ill at ease and offered only cursory efforts to have the proceedings delayed.

United States Marshal Tom Rickenbaugh informed the court that Kruger was in the process of replacing the dam that had been dynamited in response to the earlier edict of the court, and appeared to have no intention of abiding by the decision of the current court or any other.

Judge Hardwick leaned back in his chair and pondered

the information for a long moment. Finally he said, 'Enforcement of this or any edict of the court is not a matter which the court may address. The court is not a law enforcement agency. It must, therefore, fall to your responsibility, Marshal Rickenbaugh, to either enforce the court's orders, or to deputize such person or persons as you feel necessary to ensure the findings of the court are adhered to.'

'Yes sir,' the marshal replied.

The judge turned to Glass. 'It falls to your duty to inform your client, Counselor, of his obligation to cede to the will of this court or find himself in violation of federal law.'

Little was said as court was adjourned. In contrast to what Ike had expected, the entire proceeding took less than half an hour. At its conclusion, Marshal Rickenbaugh approached him and Minerva. 'Are you prepared to do whatever may become necessary to make sure this polecat don't blind-side you again?'

Ike nodded. 'I think we got it covered. It'll likely come to a fight, sooner or later, though. Kruger ain't gonna back down without a fight.'

'Well, I can't intervene until something illegal is actually done,' Rickenbaugh said with obvious regret. 'One of the frustrations of this job is that I can't prevent crime or keep anyone from gettin' killed. I can bring the people to justice that break the law, but not until after they break it. It's up to you to protect yourselves and your interests.'

'We've been workin' on coverin' that. It won't likely take Kruger long to break a law or three. Then we'll take care of it.'

110

'You have full authority to do that, once the law is broken.'

As Ike and Minerva headed back for the ranch they both knew it wouldn't take a long time for that to happen. However, they were too enraptured with each other's company and plans for their future to worry too much about it just then.

CHAPTER 17

Quite possibly they didn't know Dane Andersen and Kid Nelson were part of the U-V-Cross crew. Maybe they just didn't see them, sitting off to the side away from the others. It was an oversight they would deeply regret.

Tubby White, Slim Wilkins and Al Reynolds sat at a table in Kelsey's Saloon. With the last round of cultivating done, the corn was 'laid by'. There was nothing more to be done with it except keep it irrigated as needed, until corn-picking time. The calves were weaned. It was as close to idle time as a ranch is ever privileged to experience, so the hands were taking advantage and relaxing in town for the day.

Conversation in the bar ceased abruptly. An unnatural hush enveloped the room. The U-V-Cross hands looked around to fathom the reason. They didn't have long to wonder.

Just inside the door four of the hands from Kruger's K-K-Bar eyed them. Each of the four had a malevolent smile playing about his mouth.

'Well lookit what we got here,' Big Dan Devlin rumbled.

'We got some o' them plowboys that ride that widow woman's skirts. You boys get tired o' takin' turns on the widow, so you come to town to find somethin' better?'

Big Dan, Lester Ernst, Luke Iverson and Pat MacDougal stood with hands poised above their guns, facing the three seated hands of the U-V-Cross. The three recipients of a challenge that could not be ignored stood up from the table and fanned out. They knew they had no chance against the hired goons of Kruger's, even if they hadn't been outnumbered. It didn't matter. They had no choice. They were compelled to defend the honor and reputation of Minerva Vogel.

Out of the field of the challengers' vision, Dane and Kid stood and quietly walked around behind the four. Their three friends' faces betrayed nothing.

'Well, you boys gonna go for them guns, or you gonna run back to the widow's place an' cry in her apron 'cause you got no manhood?'

Dane stepped up behind big Dan. He grabbed him by the collar and the seat of his pants. He lifted him high over his head and took a step backward.

At Dan's startled squawk, the other three of Kruger's men turned to see what was going on. As they did so, Dane threw Big Dan into them as if he were throwing a small tree limb over a fence. Devlin smashed horizontally into the three men, driving all four to the floor in a tangled heap.

Nothing was said. Al Reynolds stepped forward and jerked Luke Iverson to his feet. Before the ruffian could even turn to face his adversary, Al looped an arm around his neck and pulled him down in a headlock. At the same time his right fist pounded into Iverson's face.

As if his fist were the piston of some steam engine, Al's right fist slammed into Iverson's face time after time after time, while his left arm kept the hapless hooligan bent over helplessly. In less than two minutes, Iverson hung limply from Al's grip, yet still the fist kept its rhythmic hammering.

At the same time that Al grabbed Iverson, Big Dan scrambled up, swinging a ham-like fist at the man who had thrown him into his fellows. Dane simply grabbed the oncoming fist with his left hand as his right fist plowed into Big Dan's face. The force of the blow picked Devlin bodily from the floor and sent him sprawling.

As he rolled, cursing, to his feet, Dane was already on him. He once again grabbed him by the collar and the seat of his pants, whirled, and slammed him into the bar, so that Devlin's face was the first thing that contacted the wooden bar top. Blood splayed outward from his broken nose and flattened lips.

Dane once again lifted the big man off the floor and shoved him, face down, on top of the bar. He grabbed a handful of hair, and began pushing the man's face on to the bar top.

Lester Ernst leaped to his feet. As he tried to figure out which of the U-V-Cross hands held the most immediate threat, Kid Nelson tapped him on the shoulder from behind. Lester whirled, right into the straight right that staggered him backward.

As he swung the fist, Kid said, 'Here he comes, Tubby.'

Responding to the cue instantly, Tubby White met the staggering Ernst with a solid right of his own, that whirled him, staggering, back to Kid. The pair used him for a punching bag, slamming him back and forth until he collapsed in an unconscious heap.

The only hand of the U-V-Cross to take a blow was Slim Wilkins. Unwilling to hammer the only opponent left to him until he was set, he faced off against Pat MacDougal. Glancing left and right, MacDougal decided he was going to be allowed to fight. With a growl he lunged forward, swinging a wild haymaker at the younger hand. Slim brushed it aside and landed a solid right of his own that stopped the onrushing Irishman in his tracks. It did little if anything more than momentarily stop his forward progress.

With three of the four K-K-Cross hands unconscious and bleeding heavily, the other four U-V-Cross hands decided to relax and enjoy the action. They sat down at one of the tables, facing the center of the floor, and crossed their legs as if engaged in some idle conversation.

MacDougal and White slugged it out in the middle of the floor for nearly ten minutes. White was clearly getting the best of the match, but MacDougal was tough and determined. He kept boring in relentlessly, immune to the number of times White had knocked him from his feet, then waited patiently for him to get up and renew his attack.

Finally Slim had his fill of it. When Pat once more rushed toward him, instead of sidestepping or backing up, Slim stepped forward to meet him. He put all the considerable strength of his brick-like build into a right hand that caught Pat squarely in the middle of his stomach. The force of the blow lifted him from his feet for an instant, and drove the wind from him. Slim stepped back half a step, then as Pat tried to straighten came back in with a right uppercut that cracked like a breaking axe handle when it landed.

MacDougal was lifted into the air, then slammed backward on to the floor. He lay spread-eagled and unmoving.

'Now why in blazes didn't you do that ten minutes ago?' Al Reynolds chided the younger cowboy.

Slim grinned. He swiped the blood from his face with the back of his hand. 'What, and miss all that fun?' he said.

'Hey, Lefty,' Al Reynolds called to the bartender. 'You got any good lye soap?'

The bartender frowned. 'Soap?'

'Yeah,' Al responded. 'I figured we oughta clean the trash outa your place for you before we leave, but it seems like it'd be fittin' an' proper, considerin' what they said, if they all woke up with a mouthful o' good lye soap.'

The bartender grinned. He fumbled around at the back-bar for a moment and returned with a large bar of P&G laundry soap. Al grinned. He picked up the bar of soap and began shaving off curls of it with his knife. 'Here ya go, boys. Pick a fella with a mouth you'd like to wash out with soap an' fill it up.'

With grins all around, the U-V-Cross hands responded. In less than a minute all four of Kruger's hands had mouths full of the substance. By the time they regained consciousness, they almost certainly would have worked their mouths enough to have the soap fairly well dissolved and thoroughly imbedded in every nook and cranny of their mouths.

When they had completed the task, Al said, 'Now let's

116

get 'em outa here so Lefty doesn't have to watch 'em blow soap bubbles.'

They dragged the four unconscious thugs outside and dumped them unceremoniously in the dirt of the street.

'You boys ready to head home or you want another drink?' Al asked.

Kid Nelson responded first. 'I wasn't done with the one I already paid for yet. I'd sorta like to have a nice quiet drink before we head back.'

'Fair enough.'

The five returned to the tables where they had been sitting when Kruger's men had arrived. They were no more than settled into place when Kruger himself burst through the door, a Colt .45 in each hand, rage emanating from his face. 'You mangy cowards have ganged up on my hands for the last time. I'm gonna kill every lowdown worthless hog-lovin''—'

He didn't get to finish the sentence. The click of twin hammers being cocked just beside him whirled his attention away from the U-V-Cross hands. He found himself staring down the twin barrels of a short-barreled twelve-gauge shotgun held by Lefty Stover.

'Put the guns away, Kruger,' he ordered. 'Now!'

Glaring alternately at the bartender and the U-V-Cross hands, Kruger sputtered for several heartbeats.

As he holstered his guns, he spat, 'You takin' up with this bunch o' vermin, Stover?'

'Yup, I sure am,' Lefty said, speaking as conversationally as if he were discussing the weather. 'But speaking o' vermin, you ain't welcome in this place. Not now. Not tomorrow. Not next week. Not ever. And that goes for every one o' them addle-brained bull moose you got workin' for you, too. Now get out, an' stay out.'

Face as purple as if he were in the midst of a fatal heart attack, Kruger snarled, 'You'll rue the day you talked to me like that. You'll rue the day.' He waggled a finger. 'Mark my words, you'll rue the day.'

He stalked out the door. Al followed him and stood watching the street.

'Whatcha lookin' at, Al?' Tubby asked.

'Just makin' sure he's leavin', instead o' waitin' to take a potshot at us when we walk out.'

'What's he doin'?'

'Tryin' to talk his boys into wakin' up.'

'Havin' any luck?'

'Yeah. They're all stirrin'. They all look like they got a mouthful o' somethin', though.'

The other four trooped to the door and crowded together to watch. It was a show worth the effort by the time the apoplectic Kruger managed to get the quartet on to their feet and headed toward the livery barn. Half an hour later the sorry procession straggled past on horseback, swaying in their saddles and spitting soapy foam with every other step of their horses. They were led by the rancher, whose rage radiated toward the watching crew of the U-V-Cross as a palpable thing.

CHAPTER 18

Dust hung heavy in the air.

'A bit of a breeze sure would be nice,' a townsman observed. 'Anything to blow away some o' this dust.'

'Ain't sure a breeze would help,' the man talking with him countered. 'Every breeze that comes along just whips up more dust. We just gotta get some rain, that's all there is to it.'

'Too late for the grass, anyway.'

'Oh, I dunno. Maybe not. One good soakin' an' the grass'll green up in a hurry.'

Both looked up as the preacher of one of the two local churches approached. 'Hey, Parson,' one of the men called out, 'how come you ain't doin' nothin' about this drought?'

'I sure would if I could,' the preacher responded.

'You're the preacher,' the other argued. 'You oughta be able to.'

The preacher shook his head. 'I wish I could. The trouble is, I'm in the sales department, not management.'

Both men chuckled at the unexpected humor. 'It does

make the sales a bit harder, though, don't it?'

The preacher frowned. 'Well, not necessarily. I've seen folks in church lately I've never seen before. The pews are filled these days. Maybe it takes hard times to make folks think about turnin' to the Lord.'

'So you're sayin' we need a drought once in a while? For purely spiritual reasons, o' course.'

The preacher smiled. 'Might be. Don't go tellin' anyone, though. I don't want it gettin' around that I'm secretly prayin' for more drought just to raise the offerings up a ways.'

'If this drought keeps up much longer, there ain't gonna be an offering at all.'

'I'm afraid that's true.'

'Say, tell me, Parson, is it true that even the bartender over at Kelsey's has been comin' to prayer meetin'?'

'Well, yeah, but that's not really a surprise.'

'It ain't?'

'He's usually in church anyway.'

'The barkeep's a churchgoer?'

'Sure.'

'You let a bartender go to your church?'

The preacher chuckled. 'Well, to start with, it isn't my church. It's the Lord's church. And it seems the Lord had a real bad habit of hanging around all the wrong people. The tax collectors, the prostitutes, the outcasts.'

Uncomfortable with the turn of the conversation, one of the townsmen said, 'Speakin' o' the bartender, I heard there was one devil of a fight over there a couple o' weeks ago.'

'So I heard.'

'I heard that bartender we was talkin' about stuck a double-barreled shotgun in Kameron Kruger's face an' told him not to set foot in there again.'

'So I heard.'

'Whatd'ya think o' that?'

The preacher shrugged. 'I don't know as I'm supposed to have an opinion on the subject. What do you think of it?'

The townsman eyed the preacher carefully for a long moment. Finally he said, 'I think it was high time somebody stood up to that guy.'

The other townsman nodded his head in the general direction of down the street. 'Speakin' o' that guy, ain't that one o' the gunmen he hired?'

The other two men turned to look. 'Yup,' the other townsman agreed. 'Nick Cadwall. I've heard of 'im. He's got a string o' killings that'd take two pages to list, according to what I've heard.'

'And fixin' to add one to it,' his companion said.

The other two looked where he was indicating. Ike Murdo had just dismounted from his horse in front of the mercantile store. 'That is not a good situation,' the preacher fretted. 'Maybe I can get between them and—'

One of the townsmen grabbed him by his sleeve and pulled him back. 'Stay out of it, Parson. Cadwall'd just as soon shoot two men as one.'

Their conversation fell to silence as the gunman called out, 'Hey you! Ain't you Murdo?'

Ike stepped away from his horse and faced the gunman, who was standing in the middle of the street maybe twenty feet from him. 'I'm Murdo,' he said.

'Then slap leather,' the gunman ordered.

Ike began to walk toward the gunman. 'I'm not wearing a gun,' he stated.

Cadwall blinked, clearly surprised and befuddled by the fact. 'You ain't heeled?'

'That should be clearly evident to a man as familiar with weapons as you appear to be.'

The gunman flushed but appeared more confused and angry than embarrassed. 'Why ain't you?'

Ike had continued approaching the belligerent gunman. 'Because if I did some lame-brained gunman might think he could achieve some sort of manhood by forcing me into a gunfight.'

'Go git a gun,' Cadwall ordered, 'or I'll shoot you down like a dog.'

'Go ahead,' Ike challenged. 'You have a good-sized audience. Do you think you could do that right here on Main Street without stretching a rope before the day's out?'

Cadwall's eyes darted left and right, noting the growing number of people gathering. They were all staying well back from the pair in the street, but all craning for a good view.

As Cadwall's eyes darted back and forth, Ike stepped in and sent a trip-hammer blow into the gunman's middle. Even less so than a normal working cowboy, the gunman was ill-equipped to withstand such a blow. The wind whooshed out of him as he doubled forward in a paroxysm of pain and breathlessness.

In what seemed a continuation of motion, Ike stepped around beside the gunman and jerked the gun from his right-hand holster with one hand at the same time as he pulled the left-hand one from its holster with the other hand. Reaching up to the man's neck he drew a large knife from between his shoulder blades. He tossed the knife on the ground. He shucked the shells out of both pistols, dropping them in the dirt. Then he spit into the end of each gun barrel and jammed them down into the dirt of the street. They both stayed there, held by the three inches of their barrels that was beneath the surface.

He stepped back around in front of the gunman. He addressed him in a calm and conversational tone. 'Now if you were to offer to fight me like a man, even though I don't even know your name or why you think you need to kill me, then I would be most happy to accommodate that wish.'

Face purple, the gunman fought to straighten up, finally able to begin sucking in huge drafts of air. 'You spit in my gun barrels,' he accused.

'Why, yes, I did,' Ike agreed. 'Then I stuck them straight down into the dirt. Now I've never actually tried it, but I've heard it rumored that if there's mud in a gun barrel when it's fired, it tends to explode. I've heard it's been known to blow a man's hand off when that happened. Not that I think you might try to shoot me in the back or anything, but I thought that might discourage the notion.'

'You're a dead man,' Cadwall asserted, beginning to regain some of his swagger. 'It's just a matter of time.'

'I'm sure you're right,' Ike agreed again. 'It's just a matter of when for each of us, isn't it? What did you say your name was?'

Glaring in helpless rage the gunman said, 'Nick

Cadwall. That name mean anything to you?'

'Hmm. Nicholas Cadwall. Would that be the same Nicholas Cadwall wanted by federal agents for war crimes committed during the war?'

'That'd be the man that's gonna kill you whenever you get guts enough to pack a gun,' he retorted.

The gunman grabbed his guns out of the dirt and looked at the ends of the barrels. He swore. He stepped over and picked his knife up out of the dirt. Ike braced himself, not sure whether he would throw the knife at him, attack him with it, or walk away.

He chose to do the latter, holding both useless guns in one hand and the knife in the other.

Ike turned to find the corpulent bulk of Justice of the Peace, Austin Church standing beside him. 'You are going to have to kill that man, you know.'

'I hope not,' Ike responded.

'He will surely kill you if you don't.'

Ike sighed heavily. 'Yeah, I wouldn't be surprised.'

It was only Henry Oldfield, owner of the mercantile store, who knew that what Ike had ridden to town for was five boxes of .45 cartridges, and four boxes of 44.40 cartridges.

It wasn't unfamiliarity with the terrain that caused Ike to ride home by a totally different route than normal.

CHAPTER 19

'Ike! Ike! Come quick!'

Ike's attention jerked from the colt he was working in the round corral. Minerva's hair and skirt were flaring behind her as she raced across the yard. She was holding a piece of paper aloft, waving it as she ran.

He hopped from the colt's back and slipped between the rails of the corral. Minerva didn't stop until she ran into him. He wrapped his arms around her to keep her from falling. Her eyes were wide, frantic. Her face was pasty as yesterday's tapioca pudding. 'Ike! He took Billy! He took Billy!'

'Whoa, whoa,' Ike soothed. 'Who took Billy? What're you talking about?'

She thrust the piece of paper into his face, too close for him to even read it. He took it and turned his body enough to hold the paper far enough away for his eyes to focus on it. His body tensed. His jaw bulged. His eyes narrowed. His lips drew to a thin tight line.

Scribbled on the paper in an uneven scrawl were the words, 'If you want to see the kid alive, be wearin' a gun.

I'll be waiting in front of Kelsey's.'

Ross Endicott had hurried from the barn at the sound of Minerva's screams. Ike silently handed him the note. He tightened the arm that was still around Minerva. 'How long ago?' he asked.

She shook her head. 'I don't know! I don't know! He was outside playing. Maverick was with him, so I wasn't worried about him.'

'When was the last time you saw 'im?'

Minerva fought to control her emotions enough to think. 'It was . . . maybe an hour ago. Maybe more. He was playing over toward the orchard.'

'Kid's on watch duty today,' Ross offered. He turned to Tubby, who had come to see what the fuss was about. 'Tub, go check on Kid.'

'Show me where,' Ike told Minerva.

Hanging on to Ike's arm as if he were the only thing keeping her from drowning, Minerva half walked, half ran around the house. They were followed by Ross and Slim who had also been drawn to the scene of obvious trouble.

Twenty yards behind the house the small orchard boasted three kinds of apple trees, two pear trees, and several cherry trees. Its shade was a welcome and safe place for a child to play. Piles of dirt with roads built around them and an assortment of wooden toys offered ample evidence of the children's creativity.

Ten feet away from the freshest signs of activity, the black and white dog lay stretched on the ground. Ike knelt and felt the animal's side, just behind his front leg. 'He's breathin',' he said.

Feeling around the limp form he quickly discovered

the lump on the side of the dog's head. As he did, the dog whimpered softly and started to stir.

'Pistol-whipped the dog so he wouldn't bite him or bark to warn anyone,' Ike surmised.

'He coulda come up into the orchard from the ravine,' Ross guessed. 'Then all he had to do was watch for a chance to grab Billy when nobody was watchin'.'

'Looks like the dog would've heard or smelled him.'

'Prob'ly did, but if he just started talkin' to Billy he'd think it was a friend. As long as Billy wasn't hollerin' or nothin', he wouldn't likely get ringy with a person.'

'Then he could clap a hand over Billy's mouth, pistol-whip the dog, and take off,' Slim offered.

'Where was the note?' Ike asked Minerva.

She pointed to the ground where the toys were scattered. 'Right there. It had a couple toys on it so it wouldn't blow away.'

'So now what do we do?' Ross demanded.

It didn't even strike Ike as strange that the foreman asked the question of him, instead of just giving orders. Since word had gotten around about Ike's past, and the relationship between him and Minerva had become more and more obvious, he had come to be more and more considered as the one to turn to. Once their official engagement was announced, he was treated as being as much owner of the ranch as she.

Ike took a deep breath. 'Might be one o' two things,' he said, sounding as if he were thinking out loud. 'He might just want me to strap on a gun and face him, so he can kill me without gettin' hung for it. In that case, all I have to do is go face 'im. But either he or Kruger might be sneakier than that. They might think I'll go gallopin' into town, with the whole crew behind me. Then they can just ride in to the ranch, take Minerva an' Minnie, an' burn the place to the ground with nobody here to stop 'em.'

Minerva gasped audibly. Ross and Tubby just stared slack-jawed, considering the possibilities. It was Ross who said, 'Or he might just be holed up in the brush by the road ready to bushwhack you on the way into town.'

They were interrupted by a pair of running horses entering the yard. 'We're out here!' Ross bellowed.

Kid Nelson and Tubby White galloped around the corner of the house and pulled their horses to a skidding halt a few feet away.

Ike was thankful for the interruption while Ross explained what they knew to the pair. Four sets of eyes turned to Ike in silent supplication for some magical answer to quell their terror. He took a deep breath. 'Well, it's most likely Cadwall that wrote the note. He's the one I publicly embarrassed by refusing to get into a gunfight with him.'

'Not to mention most o' the rest o' Kruger's men ain't in that good a shape yet,' Slim offered.

Ike shook his head. 'They're pretty well healed up by now. I'm guessin' he's got half a dozen more gunhands on the payroll by now, too. He's workin' hard to get that dam rebuilt in spite of the court order. And you know he's got guards posted all around it to keep us from blowin' it up again. That'd take more men than he had available.'

'So what are you going to do?' Minerva demanded, terror giving a harsh edge to her voice.

'I'm going to go to town,' Ike said.

The four studied him, waiting for further explanation. 'If he just wants a chance to face me, I'll have to give it to him. But it ain't likely he'll have Billy there with him. That'd be too much trouble, besides attractin' too much attention. But I have to take care of him first; then we can go get Billy.'

'Go where?' Minerva demanded.

'Ten to one he'll be at Kruger's,' Ike guessed. 'This whole thing is too snaky to be a knee-jerk reaction of a hired gun to being publicly humiliated. It's got Kruger written all over it. The easiest thing he can do to keep Billy where he wants 'im is to turn 'im over to that woman he lives with.'

'Carlotta,' Minerva identified. 'I know her. In spite of whatever she is to Kruger – she says she's his housekeeper – she wouldn't hurt Billy.'

'So why don't we just ride over there and get 'im?' Ross demanded.

Ike shook his head. 'Too risky. Cadwall has to be taken care of first. Then we'll have to slip in and get Billy before things get too wild.'

'And just how do you expect to do that?'

Ike took a deep breath. 'I'll handle figurin' that out. First I got an appointment in town.'

'Cadwall ain't apt to be alone.'

Ike bit a corner of his lip. 'He might be. His pride really needs to prove to everyone that he can take me, one on one.'

'You're just going to ride in there without even wearing a gun to meet that gunfighter?' Minerva demanded.

'That ain't exactly what I said,' Ike disputed.

He turned to Slim. 'Slim, would you get my saddle on Surprise for me. I'll be a couple minutes.'

Slim whirled and took off at a run. Ross jutted his head forward. 'I ain't lettin' you ride in there alone,' he insisted.

'That's the way it's gotta be,' Ike stated. 'If Kruger plans to use this as a chance to ride into the place without any resistance, you've got to have everybody here and be ready. And make sure your sentries are posted other places than the main road this time.'

He wheeled and walked away. Still clinging to his arm, Minerva kept pace. Ross looked after them like a child who had just been scolded by the schoolmom. Tubby and Kid were suddenly very busy with checking the stirrups on their saddles.

At the house Ike turned to face Minerva. He wrapped both arms around her, but pulled his head back so he could look down into her eyes. 'Sweetheart, just trust me. I'll take care of Cadwall, and I'll get Billy back. Just take care of Minnie, and wait. I know that's the hardest thing in the whole world to do right now, but it's what you need to do. Wait an' pray.'

All pretense and all hesitancy was gone from her as well as it was from him. She grasped both sides of his shirt, wadding the cloth in her fists, looking up into his eyes. 'Darling, I can't just sit here and wait!'

'I know it's hard,' Ike consoled her. 'But there ain't any choices right now. Just trust me. I promise I'll take care of this. Can you trust me that far?'

She choked back a sob. Tears streamed down her face. The hands that gripped the wadded sides of his shirt trembled. 'Promise?' she demanded. 'Are you sure?'

Ike took a deep breath. 'Honey, I've dealt with a lot more dangerous people than Cadwall. I know how to get into Kruger's place and get Billy. Remember, I told you there were some things that I'm really good at? This is the kind of thing I'm really good at. Trust me. Please?'

Through the tears she sobbed, 'Oh, Ike! Ike! I couldn't stand it if I lost you and Billy both. I just couldn't. I . . . I love you, Ike!'

His arms tightened around her. 'I love you too, sweet-heart. I've loved you since the first day I rode into this yard. And I love Billy too. I won't let you down.'

He kissed her quickly and turned away, praying and hoping that he hadn't just lied to the woman he loved more than life.

CHAPTER 20

Within minutes of reading the note left behind when Billy was kidnapped, Ike had emerged from the bunkhouse looking like a different man from the one known to the crew. He wore the same clothes, but he seemed to wear them differently. His bearing was different. His eyes darted everywhere, missing nothing. Some unseen force seemed to almost quiver beneath the skin, lending him an aura of a tightly wound spring that might explode at any moment.

He wore a gun nobody on the U-V-Cross had seen before. Some of the hands had heard him practice with it on occasion. More so lately than before. But they hadn't been where they could watch. What they heard was usually a single shot, followed by a pause, then another single shot, as if he were drawing and shooting. Once in a while they had heard him empty the cylinder of the pistol in a volley of shots so rapid they sounded almost like one continual blast.

It was that pistol that had first caught their eye when he stepped out to the saddled horse Tubby White held ready for him. It was a .45 Colt, low on his hip, tied down. It hung just where the palm of his hand brushed it when he stood at ease. Its grips showed the unmistakable wear of countless encounters with the palm of his hand.

On the other side of his belt hung a large Bowie knife. The hands had never seen it, either. Its haft was smooth and worn as well. It looked as if it had hung there on his belt from the beginning of time. Or from the beginning of a war he thought was far behind him.

None of them could see or sense the other knife, or the other gun concealed by his clothing.

His eyes were flat and hard, seeming out of place in a face they had all enjoyed for its twinkling eyes and ready wit.

Equally surprising was Minerva's reaction to the transition. This was the man she had fallen in love with. This was the man to whom she had unabashedly proclaimed her love. This was the man she was pledged to marry. But he was changed. He was different. He looked hard and cold and . . . and . . . dangerous!

Perhaps her reaction could be understood in the light of the fact that it was her son who had been kidnapped. Perhaps it could be understood in the light of the danger she and her whole crew faced. In truth it lay in the certainty his appearance emanated that he could do exactly what he had promised to do. He could rescue her son. He could deal with the most dangerous man Kruger could find to destroy them. To her, he seemed capable of doing anything he set out to do.

She had been standing with Tubby, trying not to betray her fear by trembling, awaiting him. When he stepped out of the bunkhouse door the merest of gasps escaped her lips. She raised her face to him. Fire flashed in her eyes. Her mouth hung open slightly, as if she were gazing on something that had suddenly filled her with awe.

Ike stopped in front of her. His voice was flat, almost without expression. 'It'll take me a couple hours to get to town and another couple back. I may be a bit slower on the way back, depending. But I'll be back.'

He turned his eyes to Ross. 'Have everyone ready to ride right about then. We'll need to move pretty fast. I'll want to be over to Kruger's just after dark, before the moon comes up.'

He started to turn to his horse, but was stopped by a small fist knotted like a piece of steel in his shirt front. Minerva stood before him, looking up into his eyes. She opened her mouth to say something, but no sound came out. Instead she stood on tiptoe and quickly planted a kiss on his lips, then turned away.

As if untouched by the act, Ike swung into the saddle. He didn't even touch the spurs to the horse's side. As always, from that first day he had ridden the big Appaloosa, Surprise seemed to read his mind. He leaped forward as if shot from a catapult. He was running flat out in three jumps. That horse could run!

There was always a chance Cadwall was waiting to shoot him out of the saddle before he ever got to town. If he thought there was a very good chance of that, though, he would have ridden a whole lot differently. Ike was confident he knew men like Cadwall well enough to predict his actions

He thinks he's the baddest gunman that ever was. Then I

humiliated him right there in the middle o' Main Street. I'm bettin' my life right now that he wants nothin' in the world as much as he wants to kill me in front of the whole town.

The brush and trees along the road became a blur passing along the corners of his eyes. His focus was far ahead, hoping to see some betraying movement if, in fact, the gunman had chosen to lie in wait.

After the first quarter mile, the horse settled into a smooth running gait. It felt to Ike as if he were floating a foot above the road. A wave of appreciation for the animal swelled up within him.

When he had stepped into the bunkhouse he had unconsciously dropped into the focus and mindset that had sustained him through the war. He had disciplined his mind to deal with the task at hand with total concentration. He did not allow his mind to dwell on images of the small boy whose life hung in the balance. He might as well have been in a different world from the woman whom he had grown to love. All that lay behind him was shut out of his awareness. Nothing existed except the road in front of him and the confrontation toward which he raced.

The sun won't be a problem, he mused. Kinda surprising he didn't try to time things so he could manage to get the sun in my eyes. Sure as anything he won't be alone, but he'll pretend to be. That balcony on the hotel would be a perfect spot for a man with a rifle. The mercantile store on the other side of the street has that lean-to on the back. It'd be plumb easy for a man to step from a saddle on to the lean-to roof, then on up to the main roof. If he was quiet, folks in the store wouldn't know he's there. He'd have a perfect firing range up and down the street, lyin' there with his rifle restin' on the ridge. Wouldn't be anything but his head

*showin'. If I come into town from this way, and Cadwall's waitin'
in front o' Kelsey's, the other two'd both be behind me. It wouldn't
matter if I beat Cadwall. I'd have at least two bullets in me before
I could draw.*

He continued to mull over the possibilities, even as his
eyes constantly probed the way ahead. Surprise was breathing hard but still running strong when he reined him in
below the top of the last hill ahead of Chickasaw.

He said 'in front o' Kelsey's,' Ike told himself for the
seventh or eighth time. *He sure ain't gonna be waitin' an'
watchin' from inside Kelsey's. Lefty banned everyone on the K-K-
Bar from his place. If he's waitin' at Hank's instead, but I end up
in front o' Kelsey's, both them guys on the roof'll be behind me.*

He nudged the heavily breathing gelding off the road.
Following the bottom of a long swale, he rode around, out
of sight of the town. He came up into the town from
behind the livery barn. He handed the reins to the surprised hostler, who had neither heard him coming nor
expected anyone from that direction. 'Give 'im a good
rubdown and a right good bait of oats, would you?' he
asked.

'Uh, yeah. Well, yeah, sure,' the hostler recovered his
aplomb. 'You sorta startled me. Say, ain't you. . . ?'

The question simply hung there as Ike stepped to the
front door. He carefully looked up and down the street.
He could just barely see the front of a hat brim in the door
that led to the hotel balcony. *Just like I thought. Waitin' back
outa sight,* he muttered silently.

The supposedly hidden man on the other side of the
street wasn't nearly as careful. Or as smart. His head and
the tall-crowned hat he wore would have been clearly

visible peering over the ridge of the roof of the mercantile store. The problem, even with that, was that Ike was already beyond where he was watching. He was on the wrong side of the roof. His whole body was clearly exposed from where Ike stood.

Following Ike's line of sight, the hostler grunted. He said, 'What's that guy doin' up there?'

Ike silently motioned him back into the livery barn. Sensing, finally, the imminent approach of violence, he ducked back inside.

Ike stepped into the middle of the street. At least all three of his adversaries should be in front of him from there. He was less than twenty feet from the front door of Kelsey's Saloon. He called out one word that echoed back from the false fronts of buildings like the shattering of a boulder. 'Cadwall!'

At the bark of his voice, the man in the doorway of the hotel's balcony whirled around, coming into full view. At the same time the one on the roof jumped and tried to whirl around and get on to the other side of the roof. His feet slipped and slid, providing a spectacle that would have been hilarious if it weren't so deadly.

Before the echoes of Ike's challenge had faded the man on the balcony jerked his rifle to his shoulder. The first shot from Ike's pistol drove him back against the door frame.

In the same motion Ike swung his gun and fired at the man on the roof. He was just lifting his rifle and trying to turn around at the same time. When the bullet from Ike's gun slammed into him he flipped over backward. All arms and flopping legs, his already dead body clattered down the roof and fell to the ground with a loud thump.

Ike whipped the gun back to the balcony. It wasn't necessary. The man there was sitting, slumped back against the door frame, his sightless eyes staring at nothing.

The entire exchange had consumed no more than three seconds. The thought raced through Ike's mind to wonder if Cadwall would even face him, one on one. He might already be hidden someplace, taking a bead on the middle of his back.

He dismissed the thought. The gunman's ego was too big to destroy his reputation by publicly shooting a man he had challenged in the back, right in the middle of town.

Ike dropped his Colt into its holster and faced the door of Kelsey's Saloon, waiting. It took nearly half a minute that seemed like at least half an hour, before Cadwall stepped out. Anger, more than fear, radiated from every part of the gunman. He crossed the boardwalk, walked to the center of the street, and turned to face Ike. 'You don't think you got a chance against me, do you?' the gunman challenged.

'You must, or you wouldn't have put two men up there to do your killin' for you.'

'I don't need any help to take care of you,' the gunman blustered.

Ike watched the gunfighter closely as he raised his voice. He well knew that every door and window along the street suddenly had multiple pairs of ears. 'Just so everybody knows,' Ike called out, 'this big brave gunfighter and the slimy snake he works for decided to kidnap a little boy to force me to face him. Then he didn't even have the guts to try to face me alone. He put two men up there to shoot

138

me down like a dog when I came after him. Let the world know forever that Nick Cadwall is a cowardly yellow dog.'

Cadwall instantly whipped his gun from its holster. He was incredibly fast. He knew it. Perhaps that explained why the look of stunned surprise spread instantly across his face as the bullet from Ike's Colt slammed into his chest and ripped a gaping hole in his heart.

His gun barely above the lip of his holster, Cadwall looked down at his own chest, then up at Ike. His eyes glazed over and went blank. He collapsed into the dirt like a tired old rag doll that had been washed a few too many times.

Ike didn't waste a look at any of the three men. He turned back into the livery barn as he thumbed the empty brass from his pistol and replaced the three cartridges he had used. 'You wouldn't happen to have a real good horse I could borrow in place of mine, would you?' he asked the hostler.

The hostler swallowed hard twice. He glanced out the door at the crumpled body of Ike's would-be assassin. His eyes darted to the roof of the mercantile store, across to the hotel balcony, then back. He swung his head around, looking back into the relative gloom of his domain. He swallowed again, then suddenly found his voice. 'My Lord!' he breathed.

He swallowed again and forced his mind to Ike's query. 'Got just the horse for ya, by gum,' he said, a flash of humor suddenly sparking in his eyes. 'Big stallion. As fine a horse as I've run across in a long while.'

'Yours?'

'Nope. Don't belong to nobody no more. I figgered

that there gunfighter had the best horse he could ever kill someone to steal, so he could always outrun any posse. He sure ain't gonna be needin' that horse no more.'

In minutes Ike had stripped saddle and bridle from Surprise and put them on to the fresh mount. Sounds of a gathering crowd were already drifting in through the front door. As he stepped into the saddle Ike said, 'My horse's name is Surprise. Take really good care of 'im. Give 'im that rubdown an' grain I asked for. I'll trade back with you first chance I get.'

He didn't wait to hear the hostler's response. He was out the back door of the livery barn before the first of the crowd ventured in the front door to see if he were there. By the time anyone thought to look out back, he was already in the swale, heading for the road back to the U-V-Cross.

He instantly applauded the hostler's appraisal. The great stallion was every bit a match for the horse he had ridden so swiftly into town. If he had bothered to look at his watch, he would have known that he had been in Chickasaw less than fifteen minutes. What he did know was that the day was far from over.

CHAPTER 21

He bit his lip. His small fists were knotted at his sides. He would not cry! He would not! He would not whimper. No matter what they did to him, he would not!

Ike's words stirred in the back of Billy's mind. 'How do you keep from bein' really scared sometimes?' Billy had asked once.

He had confided in Ike a bad dream that had left him trembling when he woke. Ike's answer had surprised him. 'You don't,' the man he had come to idolize had told him. 'You just go ahead and be scared. Just don't let bein' scared decide what you do.'

'Are you scared sometimes?'

Once again Ike's answer surprised him. 'Billy, I been scared at least half of my life.'

'So what d'ya do when you're scared?'

'Just keep your head. Keep your mouth shut and your eyes open. Remember what it is you need to do. Keep watching for a chance to do it. When you see your chance, move quick. Most times you can find a way out of even some really tight spots if you do that.'

Well, he was in a tight spot, sure enough. The guy had killed Maverick by hitting him on the head with his gun. At least, Maverick sure looked dead. Then he grabbed him with a hand over his mouth so he couldn't yell for help. He tried to bite the hand, but the guy had it clamped too tight. He couldn't even open his mouth. The guy stuck a piece of paper under some of his and Minnie's toys. Then he ran to where he had his horse tied. He got on the horse still holding him. He held him in front of him and kept his hand over his mouth. Really tight.

When they'd gone a-ways away from the house he told him, 'I can keep my hand over your mouth all the way, if I need to. If you promise you ain't gonna yell or nothin', I'll take it off. Not that anybody'll hear you now, anyway.'

The guy waited a while, then said, 'Well, you gonna promise to be quiet?'

Billy tried to talk, but couldn't. He shook his head yes as best he could. The guy took his hand off his mouth.

Boy, it felt good to be able to breathe without smellin' that guy's dirty hand. 'Where you takin' me?' he asked.

'You'll find out soon enough.'

'Why are you takin' me?'

'Cuz the boss told me to.'

'Who's the boss?'

'Kruger. Mr Kruger to you.'

'Was that a note you left where you grabbed me?'

'Yup.'

'Did you write it?'

'Nope. I don't write.'

'Who wrote it?'

'Nick.'

'Who's Nick?'

'You ask too many questions.'

'Why'd you hafta go an' kill my dog?'

'I don't reckon I kilt 'im.'

'Why'd you hit him with your gun, then?'

'To keep him quiet.'

'You still didn't tell me why you went an' took me.'

'Cuz Nick says it'll make Murdo come to town after him.'

'Why does he want Mr Ike to do that?'

'So he can kill 'im.'

Billy felt as if the whole world had slipped away, leaving the huge hole it used to occupy right in the middle of his stomach. 'Why does he want to kill Mr Ike?'

'Just shut up. No more questions.'

'But—'

'I said no more questions! You ask me one more question an' I'll clap my hand over your mouth again. Either that or rap you upside the head like I did your dog. Just shut up.'

The rest of the ride was double torture for Billy. It was far from comfortable sitting on the pommel of the guy's saddle, with one leg on each side of the saddle horn. The guy could have crowded back in his saddle and made room for him in front of him if he wanted to. He either didn't want to or wasn't smart enough to know that. Maybe he'd never had a kid riding double with him before.

He was just as miserable because he couldn't ask any questions, and Mr Ike was about to get killed. He always got to ask questions. But every time he'd think of a question and start to ask it, he'd remember Maverick. He really, really hoped the guy was right, and Maverick wasn't dead. He really loved Maverick.

Boy, his mom was really going to be mad when she found that note and he wasn't there. He wondered what the note said. Well, at least she'd know he hadn't just gone off somewhere. It wasn't his fault he was clear out of the yard where he was supposed to stay.

It seemed like a really long way before they came out on a road and he knew where they were. They were almost to Kameron Kruger's place. He recognized it because he had been there before. His mom didn't like Mr Kruger anymore, though. He was glad about that. He didn't know why, but he was afraid of Mr Kruger. It seemed like there was something mean inside him, where he didn't let it show, but if you looked in his eyes you could see it some-times.

When they rode into the ranch yard Mr Kruger was standing on the porch. The guy that had grabbed him rode up to the porch. He grabbed Billy by the back of his overalls and picked him up. He sort of set him down, sort of dropped him, on the ground. He fell down, but jumped right back up. 'Here's the kid,' the guy said.

'You left the note?'

'Put it right where the kid was playin'. I stuck a couple of his toys on it so it wouldn't blow away.'

'Anybody see ya?'

'Don't think so. Boss, I ain't sure this is too good an idea, grabbin' a kid this way.'

'I don't pay you to think,' Kruger snapped. 'Go get to work.'

The guy hesitated just a minute, then turned and rode

off across the yard.

'Carlotta!' Kruger bellowed.

Almost instantly a Mexican woman, Billy guessed was just about his mom's age – really old, anyway – came out. '¿Qué pasa?'

'Knock off the Mexican stuff. Talk English. Here. Take this kid and keep him outa sight and outa trouble.'

'Who is this boy?'

'Vogel's kid. Now take 'im inside.'

'Why do you have Señora Vogel's child?'

'You ask too many questions. Just keep 'im in the house and make dang sure you don't let 'im outa your sight.'

Clearly conflicted, Carlotta put a hand in the middle of Billy's back and shepherded him into the house. 'How did you get here to our place?' Carlotta asked in her heavy accent.

'That guy grabbed me an' stuck me on his saddle and brought me here.'

'What guy?'

'I don't know. Some guy that works for Mr Kruger.'

'What for do they want you to be here?'

'I dunno. I think it's to make Mr Ike fight somebody. Nick somebody wants to kill him.'

Carlotta studied him, clearly thinking through the implications. 'This is a very bad business,' she said finally.

'So are you going to make me stay here?' Billy demanded.

'Of course I will make you stay here. And if you try to run away, I will spank you harder than you have ever been spanked in your life. Do you understand? Or I will tell Señor Kruger, and he will do lots worse. Are you hungry?'

What foolishness to ask a 7-year-old if he's hungry. Of course he was hungry. And when Carlotta had fed him enough for three boys his size, he was also sleepy. She told him he could lie down on the floor at the edge of the kitchen. He curled up there and was sound asleep in minutes.

When he woke up the shadows were long and the light in the kitchen was dim. He looked out the window. It was already getting dark. Really dark. He hadn't intended to sleep that long.

There was a lot of yelling and talking going on in the front yard. He couldn't see Carlotta. He slipped from the kitchen, through the front room, and looked out the open door. A rider on a horse that was all foamy with sweat was talking and waving his hands. He remembered him. He was in the court with Mr Ike and his mom. The sheriff. That's who he was. He remembered the moustache. Mr Kruger acted like he was really mad. He was waving his hands around and yelling orders to his men.

Whatever was going on, it wasn't good. Billy was really scared now. He retreated to the kitchen. He had to get away. He just didn't have any idea how to go about it.

Just then Carlotta came into the kitchen. He heard her coming and lay back down and curled up, pretending to still be asleep. She barely glanced at him. She set a cast iron skillet on the edge of the stove, then began chopping up something on the table. Her back was to him.

He could almost hear Mr Ike's words. *Just keep your head. Keep your mouth shut and your eyes open. Remember what it is you need to do. Keep watching for a chance to do it. When you see your chance, move quick. Most times you can find a way out of*

146

even some really tight spots if you do that.

I need to get away from here. I have to do something though, or Carlotta won't let me get away. His eyes fell on the heavy skillet. Quick as a wink he stood up and tiptoed softly over to the stove and picked it up. It was a lot heavier than he thought it would be. He swung it back and forth a couple times. He stepped over closer behind Carlotta. He gripped the handle with both hands. He turned halfway around, then swung back, using the speed of his twist to help lift the skillet in an arc that would bring it up to the level of her head when it was going just as fast as he could make it go.

He must have made some slight noise. Carlotta made a small sound and turned around. Just as she turned, the skillet slammed into the side of her head. It flew from his hands, clattering on to the floor. Carlotta fell across the table, then rolled over on to the floor. Her eyes were closed.

The front door opened. Billy looked around frantically. The kitchen door opened into a space of twenty yards before trees and brush obscured anything beyond. It was too dark to more than just see the outline of that shelter. Billy flew through the door and raced for cover as fast as his legs would carry him.

Behind him he heard somebody yell, 'Hey! What happened?'

Then as he plunged into the brush the same voice yelled, 'Hey, boss! The kid brained Carlotta with a skillet!'

Even above the noise he made crashing blindly through the brush in the dark, he heard Kruger curse. 'Catch that kid! I don't care if you kill the little brat, just catch him!'

147

Billy soon heard the sounds of pursuit. He kept running into trees and bushes too big to push through. Then he had to back up and feel his way around. They were going to catch him. They were going to kill him. He had to run faster, but he couldn't.

Suddenly a pair of hands grabbed him and lifted him off the ground. He kicked and squirmed, but the arm that went around him held him like a vise. A loud grunt from behind him was followed by brush breaking. Then there was silence. He braced himself to die.

CHAPTER 22

Ross ordered three of the hands to stay at the ranch, just in case Kruger was trying to outsmart them. At Ike's suggestion, they made a quick haystack in the middle of the big corral. At the edge they put a glass jug of kerosene with a candle stuffed in the mouth of it. He lit the candle.

'Just in case they do spring a surprise attack, shoot the jug of coal oil,' Ike instructed. 'That'll light the haystack. We'll be able to see the glow from it pertnear to Kruger's, but it won't catch anything else on fire.'

It was a precaution he was pretty sure was unnecessary, but he hadn't made it all the way through a war without taking unlikely possibilities into account.

That left six of them to take on Kruger's crew on his own ground. It was not going to be an easy task. Even harder would be making sure he had Billy safe before they attacked.

There was no thought in his mind that it was anything less than all-out war at this point. The kidnapping of a child removed all hesitancy, all doubt, all restraint.

They rode as swiftly as they could in the gathering darkness. By the time they were half a mile from Kruger's it was pitch dark. The moon wouldn't rise for nearly an hour. When it did, though, they would have plenty light to shoot by. They needed to be in place and ready when that time came.

'Pull up here,' Ike said softly. 'I'll go on foot from here. When I get back with Billy, we'll spread out and get in place so we're ready to do what we gotta as soon as the moon's up.'

'You goin' in there by yourself?' Ross demanded, trying to keep his voice low.

It was too dark for him to see Ike nod. 'I can do it by myself. More than one will make too much noise.'

'But you don't even know where they're keepin' 'im.'

'He'll have to be in the house.'

'Gettin' that close to the house by yourself is plumb suicide.'

Again the foreman couldn't see Ike shake his head. 'It's dark. They'll have to have a lamp lit inside, especially if they're not expectin' anyone to come up through the timber. That gives me all the advantage.'

Ross would have argued further, but Ike simply melted silently into the darkness, leaving the foreman holding the reins of the third horse Ike had ridden that day.

Ike had never said anything about it, but he had scouted Kruger's ranch buildings and surrounding terrain on his own, not long after the current conflict began. He had ridden into the yard blind the first time, with just Ross to back him. He hadn't had a choice then. He knew from long experience that knowing the terrain was essential. He wasn't going to go in blind a second time.

He made his way as swiftly and silently as he could on a beeline toward the ranch house. He was still a good hundred yards from it when a door slammed. Less than a minute after the door slammed, brush began to rustle and break as someone crashed blindly through it. He frowned.

Distinctly on the night air, a startled voice cried out, 'Hey, boss! The kid brained Carlotta with a skillet!'

Ike stopped dead in his tracks. He grinned into the darkness. The grin was replaced almost instantly. His lips drew to a thin line. His eyes flashed, as he heard Kruger's voice yell, 'Catch that kid! I don't care if you kill the little brat, just catch him!'

He instantly connected the sounds of flight and pursuit through the brush and moved to intercept them. In two minutes he felt, rather than saw, Billy moving toward him, crashing his way through the brush. He reached out and grabbed him, lifting him off his feet. With one arm he held the boy tightly against himself. The other flashed as starlight caught a faint gleam from steel zipping through the darkness. A startled grunt was followed by the sound of something heavy landing on the ground. Silence settled around them.

Billy kept trying his best to squirm loose. Ike put his mouth close to the boy's ear and whispered, 'Billy! Billy! It's me. You're OK now.'

He went stiff and stopped squirming. As Ike loosened his grip, he twisted his head and tried to see his rescuer. Instead of yelling as he wanted to, he whispered, 'Mr Ike? That you?'

'Yeah it's me, Billy. You're OK now.'

He stood the boy on the ground. Billy gripped his trouser leg tightly. 'Where's the guy that was chasin' me?'

'Dead.'

Silence engulfed them. An awed whisper broke it. 'Dead?'

'Yeah.'

'Who kilt 'im?'

'I did.'

'How?'

'Never mind. Stand still and don't move till I get back.'

He disappeared into the darkness. Panic rose in Billy's throat. He swallowed hard, trying to force it down. He crouched down close to the ground and forced himself to wait like Ike had told him.

Close by he heard someone moving slowly and cautiously through the brush. A voice carried on the breeze, 'Where you at, Luke?'

Then, 'What's goin' on?'

When there was no answer, 'You get the kid?'

A startled grunt was followed by a sudden brief crashing of brush. Silence returned.

Billy fought the urge to try to run. He remembered how much the brush hurt as it lashed across his face and arms as he had fled, running blindly through it. He knew Ike had told him to stay put. He was almost ready to flee anyway, when Ike was there again, almost against him. He bent over and used grass and leaves to clean something off the blade of a big knife. Then he put it in its sheath on his belt. Billy hadn't ever seen the knife or sheath before.

'Let's move,' he whispered. 'Stay as quiet as you can.'

Billy couldn't understand it. Somehow in the dark Mr

Ike was able to steer him around the bushes and trees, so he didn't get scratched hardly at all, as long as he held on to his hand. He told himself that was the reason he clung to it so tightly.

It seemed to the lad to be a long way until he heard a horse blow softly. Then he heard a saddle creak. A bit ring jingled. 'We're comin' in,' Ike called softly.

'You find where he is?' Ross Endicott's voice answered.

'He's with me.'

'You got Billy?'

'I'm right here, Mr Endicott,' Billy answered, trying to speak softly.

'How'd you get him outa there?' Ross demanded of Ike.

Ike almost chuckled. 'I didn't. There just wasn't anyone there to protect them from Billy.'

'Whatd'ya mean?'

'The Mexican woman was supposed to be watchin' 'im. Billy laid her out with an iron skillet and ran.'

Dead silence waited for the punchline to some joke. Nothing came.

Ike's voice was imperious, and delayed until later any explanations. 'I don't want Billy where he might catch a stray bullet. Leroy, you stay here with him and the horses. The rest of you follow me as quiet as you can.'

Nobody challenged his right to be giving the orders, including the foreman. They filed back into the timber, moving single file behind Ike.

When they were close, Ike stopped. They grouped close around him. He spoke softly, little above a whisper. 'The moon's comin' up now. It'll be a full moon, an' light enough to shoot by in fifteen or twenty minutes. The ranch house is right ahead of us. You might stumble over a couple guys lyin' in the brush. Don't worry about them. They're dead. I don't know how many other hands Kruger has, but they'll know we're here and comin' after 'em. Billy said the sheriff is there too. Even if they haven't found the two that are dead, they'll know they were chasin' Billy an' didn't come back. Ross, you and Kid swing around to the left and cover the bunkhouse. Dane and I'll go straight and get to where we can see both the front and back doors of the house. Al, you go farther to the right to where you can cover the barn and corral. Everybody get in place and get laid flat where you've got a good field of fire. Stay flat and shoot from there when the lead starts flyin'. You're a lot harder to hit when you're flat on the ground. When it's time, I'll yell for Kruger to give himself up.'

'You don't want nobody circlin' around to the other side?' Ross asked.

Ike shook his head. 'There's nothin' around there anyone's likely to head for, and if we're all on one side we're not gonna be shootin' toward each other.'

The logic of it seemed unarguable, so nobody commented. Instead each man began to move as quietly as possible toward his assigned position. They would probably need to move a little when it got light enough to see, but they'd be close to their assigned places.

Dane followed Ike silently to a spot Ike designated. It was just growing light enough Dane could see him point to the base of a large tree. It was less than fifty feet from the end of the ranch house. Dane could clearly see the back door, and to within a few feet of the front door. Ike moved to his left, to a position that commanded an unobstructed view of the front door. They settled in to wait.

There were no lamps showing any place. Unnatural stillness draped the yard and buildings. The K-K-Bar crew had to know by now that their hostage was gone, and they were about to be attacked. Nerves had to be frayed. A low buzz of conversation started several times, but was swiftly silenced.

An owl hooted to frighten some small woodland creature into a startled movement. Its effectiveness was borne witness by the whisper of air past swooping wings, then their pumping against the air as the predator soared with a fresh morsel of food in its talons.

The wind soughed softly in the treetops. Far off, a coyote yelped several times, with the yelps ending in a protracted howl that hung in the thin air. It was followed half a minute later by an answering howl from some nearer hilltop.

The soft scuffing of a boot against something betrayed the position of somebody that waited for the expected attack.

Inside the house a floor creaked.

Slowly the deep darkness gave way to a soft silver light. It laid a false sense of serenity across a scene pregnant with a violence ready to erupt. Still the peace and silence held.

The tip of the moon appeared above the mountains, looking red and ominous. It seemed strange that a moon so red would cast a light so softly silver. Yet the silvery light grew and expanded until trees and buildings began to draw their own shadows on the canvas of ground. Still no sound rose to disturb the scene.

The moon slowly continued its climb, working to extricate itself from the damping cover of the mountains. Eyes grown used to near total darkness were able to pick out shapes and forms, and soon to see nearly as well as if it were daylight.

Causing even his own men to jump, Ike's voice boomed out. 'Kruger! You're surrounded. You're under arrest for kidnapping. Throw out your guns and come out with your hands up.'

For the barest instant silence draped its gossamer veil over the scene again. That silence was ripped apart by a dozen gunshots ripping into the trees and brush.

Answering fire came at once from five places that seemed like a dozen to those who truly believed they must be surrounded by a great posse. Two men almost immediately called out, 'I'm hit! I'm hit!'

The unmistakable *thunk* of a bullet smacking into living flesh indicated another that wouldn't be announcing the 'hit' that caused his sudden demise.

Glass shattered from windows in both the house and bunkhouse.

From the barn a voice called, 'Don't shoot! I'm puttin' my gun down. I got nothin' to do with no kidnappin'.'

Silence followed the announcement. Four other voices quickly added their disclaimer and surrender.

'Walk out in the yard with your hands in the air, then,' Ike yelled.

From between the rails of the corral, from the barn, from the bunkhouse, six men began to walk into the open, hands held high.

'That's far enough!' Ike called.

They stopped, looking scared and uncertain.

'Get ready,' Ike said softly. 'Move six feet to your right, but keep your head down.'

At the same time he moved as many feet to his own left. Still able to talk softly and know Dane could hear him, he said, 'Kruger's been linin' up on the sound of my voice. He's gonna come out shootin' any time.'

The words were no sooner spoken than done. At an evidently shared signal, Lester Ernst burst through the front door, a Colt in each hand, firing rapidly at the position he had concluded Ike was speaking from. At the same instant Kruger rushed out the back door, also firing from first one hand and then the other, at the same spot.

Kruger managed to get off a combined four shots before he was folded up in the middle and thrown back three feet by twin blasts of double-ought buckshot from Dane's twelve-gauge shotgun.

Ernst nearly emptied both guns before he was stopped dead in his tracks by a bullet from Ike's .45 tearing through his throat. Its exit shattered his spine at the base of the skull, instantly paralyzing his entire body. He never knew he died before he hit the ground.

The group of men in the yard hoisted their sagging arms higher in the air, clearly signaling that they were out of the fight.

'I come out now,' a woman's voice called from the kitchen.

'Come on,' Dane replied.

Carlotta staggered out the door, grabbing a post that supported the small roof over the back porch to keep from falling. The left side of her face was grotesquely swollen and discolored. 'I sit down now,' she slurred, slumping down on to the top step. 'I tell him you can't take no kid like that. He no listen to Carlotta. I think maybe I try to protect boy from him. Nobody protect Carlotta from that boy.'

Ike called across the yard. 'Al, Kid, check the house, bunkhouse, and barn. Make sure nobody's hidin' out. Ross an' Dane'll watch your backs.'

It took minutes to ensure that nobody was hiding anywhere. 'Pile all the guns in the yard, well away from them guys,' he ordered.

When that was completed he addressed the group. 'Who grabbed the boy?'

Silence hung heavily for several seconds. Finally one of the group said, 'Luke. But he didn't wanta. He tried to tell Kruger it'd make all hell bust loose.'

He looked around as if expecting a bullet from somewhere for his willingness to tell. When nothing happened he said, 'Where is Luke?'

Ike said, 'He tried to grab the boy a second time. He caught up to 'im out there in the brush. He didn't survive.'

Once again a fierce and unbreakable silence clamped every tongue. Friend and foe alike stood with jaws agape, staring at Ike. Finally one of Kruger's men said, 'I know the kid nailed Carlotta with a fryin' pan. But Luke. . .? The kid didn't really kill Luke, did he?'

Some twisted sense of humor kept Ike from even answering the question. He just let it hang for a long moment. After a while he said, 'You boys gather your stuff, saddle up, and ride outa this country. If I see any one of you ever again, I'll shoot you down on sight like a rabid coyote.'

Once again there was an instant of hushed hesitation. And then, as one, five men lowered their hands and headed for the bunkhouse. 'Al, Kid, watch 'em.'

He didn't think there was any need for caution. He was sure the idea of a deadly seven-year-old boy out there somewhere would keep them moving for a long way. He wasn't sure whether Minerva would like the idea of a myth like that growing up around her son. He just might wait to share that part of the story with her until after a honeymoon he was already planning in his mind.